AF428423

LITTLE FOXES

Melani Redmiles-Quinley

Printed in the United States of
America

First Printing, 2023

ISBN 979-8-9897668-2-6

This is fiction…but also not.
It is for the crime-obsessed warriors.
Those who are haunted by the darkness,
chasing that ultimate fix – justice served.

But, above all, it is for them…the ones
who never made it home.

Chapter 1

She sits at the vanity staring at her dull, tired eyes in the mirror. Her pupils look so small. They remind her of herself, surrounded by a vast, never-ending blue. She unconsciously rubs a ragged scar on her upper left arm. The loud ear-shattering sound of the kitchen phone shoots like a bullet through her small apartment, startling her back into reality. Who still has a landline, she thinks? The thirty-something-year-old woman staring at herself in the mirror for... how long has it been? The one whose overexcited mother is so worried about her that she insists on being able to contact her at all times in all the possible ways. She is surprised her mother hasn't made her learn how to send smoke signals yet, just in case.

She lets it go to voicemail but listens as she prepares her coffee at the kitchen counter. It is, of course, her mother. Who else calls her on this thing? The sound of her mother's voice fills the apartment as she takes slow sips of her coffee. She drinks it black and straight from the pot. It burns the roof of her mouth, and she holds it there before swallowing, savoring it.

"Mable has taken to painting all of us. She sets up shop right in her front yard and just paints us all day long! Can you believe it?" Mable is her mother's eccentric neighbor in the retirement community where she lives, and yes, she can believe it. All the people there are way too into each other's businesses. "I thought about what you asked me to do the other day," her mother continues. "And well, I just don't see the point in going there and seeing that man…and I wish you wouldn't either. I am not sure why you are hashing up old memories from so long ago. You know, I read an interesting article recently about how unhealthy it is to dwell on negative things. It said something about positive reflection…or positive recollection…what was it? Oh, I can't remember. I'll just email you the article, even though you probably won't read it." There is a man's muffled voice in the background—Stan, her mother's husband. "Okay, okay, I'm almost done," her mother says. "Just think about it, honey. And please call me back soon, before I worry."

She listens for the soft click. Her mother always hangs up the phone very delicately. The silence that ensues is almost deafening. She thinks about what her mother said about not dwelling on the past. She means well, but she doesn't understand that this will never be over until she has closure. As she finishes her coffee, she stares at a calendar hanging on the wall. Some of the days are crossed out with big red X's, but there is one, two weeks from today, which is circled multiple times with the word TRIAL written in large red, all-capital letters. It is the day she's been waiting for since her life changed all those years ago when she was a child. It is her closure.

Chapter 2

The two girls walk along the sidewalk, hand in hand. Michelle- 12 years old- is wearing glasses that look too large for her face. Her shaggy blonde bangs overlap the thick brown frames. She pulls her younger sister, Laura- 10 years old- along beside her. Laura is a foot shorter than Michelle, with light hair that is almost white. She walks leisurely beside her sister, lost in thought. "Come on Lor, walk faster", urges Michelle.

"Don't pull me, Shell", Laura whines, "Why are you in such a hurry?"

"Cause it's Easter weekend. The mall is gonna close early and we won't have much time to look at stuff if we don't hurry."

"It's morning. It won't close for hours", whines Laura.

Michelle just rolls her eyes in response.

"Shelly! Over here, slowpoke!" Two girls yell and wave their arms from a short distance away from them.

Michelle drops Laura's hand quickly. The two girls come barreling towards them, practically knocking Michelle off her feet. "What time did you two get here? The crack of dawn?"

LITTLE FOXES

"Yeah, almost, but we got to see Ron Leberman open up the pretzel cart and you missed it!"

Michelle mimes an arrow being shot through her heart and feigns dying, falling into the arms of the two girls.

"Hello Dawn…Hello Julie," interrupts Laura.

The brown-haired girl, Dawn, smiles at her and gives her a little wave. The red-headed girl, Julie, remains apathetic, smirking down at her.

The three older girls fall in step with one another. Laura walks behind them, listening silently to their chatter about school and boys. She absentmindedly touches the braided bracelet tied around her wrist, as she walks. The purple and blue threads woven tightly together calm her. Reminding her of the day her sister made it for her.

The mall is abuzz with shoppers. There are Easter decorations everywhere as well as the word SALE, written in large block letters. The girls rip through the stores like tornadoes, looking at everything and leaving a trail of energy and recklessness behind them.

When they get to a store called Craft Connection, Laura walks leisurely through the aisles of colorful yarns and fabrics, touching each one delicately. Michelle finds her holding a fabric sample up to her cheek. "There you are," she says. "Is it soft?" Laura nods and brushes the fabric lightly across Michelle's face. Michelle closes her eyes and smiles. "I promise we won't stay too much longer. Julie and Dawn just want to check out a few more stores, okay?"

Laura pushes out her bottom lip. "I wish it was just us."

Michelle gently strokes the hair out of Laura's face. "What if we get milkshakes?"

Laura grins in reply.

She sucks on the straw. Her cheeks turn red with exertion as she tries to draw the thick liquid through.

Julie laughs at Laura. "Slow down there, man-eater." Dawn shoots Julie a sideways warning glance. "What," retorts Julie. "She's really going at it."

Laura looks up at Michelle, confused about the term man-eater, but Michelle's focus is somewhere else. She is looking across the food court with a curious expression on her face.

A man is standing several feet away from their table, near the restrooms. He is staring at them without breaking his gaze. "Is that guy looking at us," asks Michelle.

LITTLE FOXES

"What guy? Is he cute," asks Julie, twisting her body in her seat to get a better look. "Oh", she says, disappointed, "The loser probably just wishes he was Laura's milkshake".

Laura doesn't understand the comment, but her cheeks burn red with embarrassment, nonetheless.

"Shut up," says Dawn, half-laughing. "He really is staring. He doesn't even care that we can obviously see him.

"Who is he staring at," asks Michelle.

"Who cares," says Julie flippantly.

"Should we do something," asks Dawn. "I mean should we like, tell an adult, or something?"

Julie stands, pushing her chair back. It scrapes against the floor with a loud screech. "Geez, I have to do everything, don't I," she says. She takes a long swig of her milkshake, slamming it back down on the table in a bold display of last- minute courage. She stops about two feet in front of the man and shouts, so everyone around can hear, "Hey Pervert. You like staring at sweet little girls?"

The man breaks his gaze, seemingly embarrassed for the first time. Then, he just walks away.

LITTLE FOXES

"Yeah, that's right, go on, get out of here…Pervert!" Julie turns and walks back to the group. She and Dawn clutch one another, almost falling from laughter.

The man, however, turns to look back one last time before disappearing out of sight. Laura grabs hold of Michelle's hand instinctively.

This time, Michelle lets her hold it.

Chapter 3

Later that evening:

"Michelle! Laura! It's dinnertime!" Marie Fox stands with her body half-in, half-out of the back door of her house. She cranes her neck to scan the backyard, looking for her daughters. She rubs her temples, wearily. The house has been blissfully quiet all day. She has a tension headache, which is why she was happy that her daughters had wanted to go to the mall this morning. "Where are those silly little foxes," she asks to herself, returning inside the house. She searches the girls' bedrooms and then the front yard without any luck. A thought begins to creep into her mind like a snake through grass. Did they ever come home?

Of course they did, she thinks, shaking it away. She searches the rest of the house, including the dusty attic. When they aren't there, she searches every nook and cranny they used to hide in when they were little.

Her head pounds harder, making her eyes sting with heat and tears. The thought returns, louder this time, until she can't hear anything else. The words in her head begin to twist from Did they ever come home, into, they never came home.

Marie tries to steady her hands while she searches through the kitchen drawers for the phone book. When she finds it, she frantically pulls it open, giving herself a paper cut in the process. She finds the number for Michelle's friend, Julie's house first. She dials but then swears to herself when the voicemail message plays. She hangs up the phone abruptly, realizing she doesn't even know what to say.

She searches the phone book again for Dawn's number. A woman, Dawn's mother, answers on the third ring. "Hello Claire," Marie says quickly, taking control of the conversation to avoid small talk. "I'm sorry to bother you during dinner, but…well…. have you seen my girls, Michelle and Laura?"

There is a brief pause on the other end of the line. "I'm not quite sure what you mean," says Claire, "aren't they home with you? I know they went to the mall with Dawn this morning." "Dawn! Dawn! Come here please." Marie listens as Claire calls for her daughter. She sucks in a deep breath and holds it in her lungs. The breath hitches and forms into a lump in her throat when she hears Dawn respond a moment later.

"What is it, Mom!"

LITTLE FOXES

"Do you know where your friend Michelle and her younger sister Laura are?" Marie can hear the obvious relief in Claire's voice as she speaks to her not missing, very much in one piece, daughter. She hates her for it.

"I don't know. We left the mall like hours ago…. Why?" The sound suddenly becomes muffled. A few moments later, Claire's voice returns.

Her voice starts to sound like background noise, as Marie listens to her speak. She is hyper-aware of her breathing and the fact that she can't seem to remember how to do it.

When Brian fox enters the room, Marie looks up at her husband. He is in his late thirties, with sandy-brown hair and a matching sandy mustache, which he always keeps trimmed in a neat curve above his mouth. It adds a somewhat comical effect to the odd expression that his face is making at her right now.

Chapter 4

Brian fox walks through the door after working all day. The first thing he sees is his wife standing in the kitchen with the phone in her hand. There is a phone book - ripped and checkered with small dots of blood - laying haphazardly on the floor next to her. Panic sets in when he registers her hands, which are gripping the phone and also smeared with blood. "What happened! Why are you bleeding," he demands.

She looks down, in a daze. I think I need to sit", she says, sliding down the wall until she is sitting on the floor.

Brian suddenly notices the yelling coming through the phone. He picks it up and, with shaking hands, brings it up to his ear. "Hello?"

There is a sigh of relief on the other end. "Oh, my goodness! Brian, thank God. Is Marie alright? She just made a noise and stopped talking after I told her what Dawn said about your daughters."

"What did she say…about my daughters?"

"Oh… well, Marie was looking for them and I just told her that Dawn hasn't seen them for three or four hours…since the mall."

Chapter 5

She lifts the weight up to her collarbone, resting it there momentarily before dropping it with measured movements. She moves the weight to her other hand and repeats the motion. Sweat runs down her face, but she doesn't wipe it away. Instead, she holds the weight a little longer, letting the sweat and discomfort soak into her skin. She continues working out until every muscle and tendon in her body aches with pleasure. This is why she keeps coming back. For this moment. This pain.

She always ends up closing her eyes when she works out. Even when the gym is crowded with other people. When she opens them today, she makes eye contact for a moment with an attractive guy, around her age. He averts his eyes, but she already caught the look. She sucked him in with her mysterious intensity and now he's intrigued. She has a feeling that this won't be the last she sees of him, but if she wants to seal the deal, it would be better to keep up the mystery. She slips away, disappearing to the locker room before he can steal another glance in her direction.

Chapter 6

"Who ever heard of seeds in a salad?" Her mother holds up a forkful of lettuce, studying it in search of seeds, with an intensity so deep, you would think she was solving one of life's great mysteries. Anything is more important than having a real conversation with her broken daughter.

"Mom, did you hear what I just asked you? I do wish you'd reconsider coming to the trial with me. I think it could be good for both of us to deal with this. Plus, it would be nice to have you there, I could use the support…because…mom, are you listening?"

Her mother slams down her fork with a little too much force, sending a piece of soggy lettuce flying onto the table behind them. "Yes, La-- sorry, Abby. I am listening and I'm hearing you ask me the same thing over and over when I've already told you I don't want to go!"

"Sorry for the name slip up," she says more quietly. "But, FYI, that is one thing that I've patiently supported you through, even though I don't understand why you had to change it. I gave you that name." Her mother crosses her arms across her chest and visibly pouts.

LITTLE FOXES

Abby folds her own arms across her chest in defiance. Why does her mother always have to twist everything, making herself into the victim?

"Hello, my name is Oscar", a man interrupts in a soft-spoken voice. "I am the head chef. I heard there was some dissatisfaction with your salad, Miss?"

Abby looks up and is startled to see the attractive guy from the gym standing beside their table. She can't tell if he recognizes her too.

What she can tell is that her mother is quite taken with this mysterious stranger and his charming demeanor. "Well, y...yes", she stammers. "There are seeds in it."

"Ah yes, fennel seeds he says. Besides being tasty, they are very good for the skin and have been known to prevent wrinkles. Not that a lovely young woman such as yourself would need any help in that department. Let me take it away and make you a new, seedless, salad right away." He lifts the plate with graceful finesse and begins to walk away, when her mother stops him.

"You know, on second thought, I think they were beginning to grow on me," she says, touching her scarf nervously, like a schoolgirl.

He sets the plate back down in front of her. "As you wish, but I insist on having the bartender make you a mojito, on the house…as well as one for your…sister?" He turns to Abby and winks mischievously.

"This is my daughter, Abigail," her mother says in a giggly way as if she's speaking to a long-lost lover.

"A drink for Abigail, then, as well", he says beaming down at her as if he's uncovered her darkest secret.

Abby didn't plan on moving things along with him like this, but her mother is making her so tense, she needs a diversion, and it would also be nice to take him off guard and re-gain some of her power.

"What a nice young man," exclaims her mother, after he leaves.

"Yes, emphasis on young," says Abby, standing. "I'm going to the restroom."

She catches up to Oscar, grabbing his arm and pulling him into a hallway. She pushes him against the wall. His face is wild with surprise. She starts kissing him. Softly at first, letting it build in intensity until she can feel him touching her, wanting her. Then, she breaks away.

She takes out her phone and pushes it into his hands. "Put your number in," she demands. He does as he's told. That's right, I'm in charge, she thinks. She walks away feeling much better, like she can take on her mother and the rest of the day.

Chapter 7

The sound wakes her from her nap. It gets louder, as her dreams fade away and her weary eyes adjust to the light. She rolls over onto her stomach and scoots to the edge of the bed. She grasps the mattress with her chubby fingers and lets her legs hang down off the side of the bed. She shimmies down, little by little, until her feet reach the floor.

She walks on shaky legs, towards the noise. It sounds like an animal, wailing in pain. It's coming from the living room, downstairs. She looks down at the steps, looming before her. The noise starts up again. She can tell now that it's her mother crying, screaming almost. Her wobbly child legs descend the old rickety stairs carefully. One at a time.

It feels like it takes forever, but she finally reaches the bottom. She collapses there, exhausted. She rolls onto her side and can see her mother sobbing on the couch. A uniformed police officer stands a few feet away, looking very uncomfortable. When he looks over and sees her laying on the floor, he smiles at her and waves. She feels an uncertainty growing in her stomach, but his face is kind, so she smiles back.

Chapter 8

Abby sits on her couch in the dark, watching re-runs of some reality TV show. Her eyelids feel heavy and begin to close. She is suddenly jolted upright by hands covering her nose and mouth. She panics, kicking her legs and flailing her arms around while rocking her body back and forth. She can't breathe. Then, the hands move from her face to her head, pushing her down, and slamming her head on the hard, wooden coffee table. She falls to the floor, darkness seeping into the corners of her vision. Two muddy boots stand in front of her and...everything goes black.

A moment later, she jolts awake. She is back on the couch safe and sound. She reaches up to touch her forehead. Nothing. Of course, it was another fucking nightmare. She gets up and goes to the kitchen and starts brewing some more coffee. She picks up her cell phone from the kitchen counter. When she unlocks the screen, it opens up to her latest contact entry. The name is OscarLoves FennelSeeds. She looks at the stove clock. 2:15 AM. She sends him a text. He responds seconds later. He's up late, like her. Good.

LITTLE FOXES

As soon as he enters her apartment, she is on him, removing pieces of clothing. They pass by her office, and he pauses. "Is this your office?", he asks. "You know, I don't even know what you do."

She pushes the office door shut. "Nothing, I work from home," she says and then goes back to kissing his neck. She guides him to the bedroom and pulls him onto the bed.

Chapter 9

She sniffs the ground. The dewy grass sticks to the palms of her hands and her bare knees. She sniffs at the air. The scent of hamburgers and hotdogs wafts towards her, making her stomach growl. She looks towards her father's legs. The apron he is wearing ruffles in the breeze as he stands in front of the grill. She knows that it says, Kiss the cook. It makes her smile because she remembers how excited he was when he got it. "Now you have to kiss me when I grill," he had said, scooping her mom into his arms. "Even if I'm all smokey."

Her stomach growls again, even louder this time. Her dad smiles down at her. She feels his love, like warmth from a radiator. "Does the puppy dog want a burger?" She pushes her tongue out of her mouth and pants excitedly. She throws her head back, looking up at the summer sky, and howls.

Chapter 10

It takes her a few moments to remember whose flesh is pressed up against her. She smiles and stretches. She sleeps the best after sex. She slips noiselessly from the bed. She puts on his shirt and tiptoes from the bedroom to her office, careful not to make a sound. It's really just a second bedroom, turned into an office.

She pauses to listen for noises and then walks over to the closet. She pushes open the doors to reveal a bunch of coats, hanging neatly on hangars.

She parts the coats in the center and pushes them to the side, just a little, in each direction. Then she stands on tiptoes and pulls the chain above her, turning on the closet light. There are photos stuck to the wall with thumbtacks.

Red yarn reaches out from the photos like a web. In the center, there is a photo of a middle – aged man. It is a mugshot. He is holding a black sign with a name on it—Gregory Lee Conrad. Above his photo, connected to him through a line of red yarn, are the photos of two young girls, side by side. They both have the same wispy, blonde hair. There are names written beneath the photos. The older girl is Michelle Fox, and the younger is Laura Fox.

Chapter 11

The Fox residence is buzzing with activity. People have been coming
and going all day. Marie, with the help of the police, has organized a
search grid. The response from friends and community volunteers
has been overwhelming. Brian Fox doesn't know half of these
people, but he is grateful for their help, and for having an excuse to
keep busy. A reason to get out of bed in the morning.

The two girls, aged twelve and ten, are said to have been last seen
hanging out with friends at the Turner Hill Mall. Sources say that
police are looking for a young man in his late teens to early twenties
who may have been interviewing…Brian switches off the TV, cutting
off the voice of the news reporter. He covers his wife, sleeping on
the couch in front of the TV, with a blanket.

He looks at the clock on the mantel. Midnight. It's been a long day,
but he still has more to do. He puts on his jacket and slips out of the
house.

Brian drives down the lonely street. His eyelids lay heavy as he stares
at the blue tinted road in front of him. The rain sits in puddles along

the sidewalk, as he scans for any movement. Anything suspicious. Anything at all…

He is jolted awake by the sound of a car horn. The car passes him impatiently. He grips the wheel tighter and pulls over to an embankment. Okay Brian, he thinks to himself. You can have one hour of sleep…then back to searching.

Chapter 12

Abby sits in her car. She is pulled up to the curb inside a cul-de-sac. The night is cold, and she is bundled up in a giant wool blanket, shivering and perusing her social media accounts on her phone while she waits. She watches as her breath comes out like smoke in front of her face and retreats further into the blanket with a shiver.

A man emerges from a house, diagonal to where she is parked, and she perks up. It is an elderly man. He is pushing a large trash bin out to the curb. Abby watches keenly as he struggles with the bin, as if it's the most interesting thing she's ever seen.

At the end of the curb, the man lingers for a moment, looking out at the quiet, empty street. When he turns his face in Abby's direction, she shrinks down into the seat. She knows he can't see her inside the blackness of her car, but, in these moments, she still always feels as though he is looking right at her. Then, he turns and walks somberly back into the house. A gloom is left behind him, thick and cold, like the darkness of the night air.

Just then, her phone vibrates on the dashboard where she set it down. She pulls her arms free of the restricting blanket and looks at the screen. She has a new message, from Oscar. It reads "Eggplant emoji or Chicken emoji?"

She smiles and types back, "kinky. didn't know u had it in u."

His replies come moments later.

"Eggplant or chicken parm?"

"Didn't know if you were vegetarian."

"I want to cook for you."

Abby inhales sharply. She doesn't usually do the whole 'relationship' thing. It's too hard to hide her secrets, and eventually when it all comes tumbling out everywhere, the other person tends to freak out, leaving her lonelier and more damaged than she was before.

Casual is what has served her well for the past few years. Yet, at the same time, she thinks of his warm smile and there is a part of her that wants to let him in. Let him cook for her, wrap her up in his arms, keep her safe. Before she can think twice about it, she types in "surprise me" and clicks send.

She throws the phone down on the seat next to her and starts up her car's engine. That's enough for tonight.

LITTLE FOXES

She turns the car around in the roundabout, driving in front of the house that the man came out of. As she passes, she slows down and rolls down the window. She sticks her arm out into the icy cold air and grazes the mailbox as she glides by with her fingertips. It has the name Fox written on it in curvy artistic letters. Then she speeds up, leaving the mailbox, the house and the desolate street behind.

Chapter 13

They sit in front of the computer screen absorbing the faces of his many victims. They feel kinship with all of them. They are damaged, like them. Damaged by him.

The anger is welling up inside them and becoming too much to bear, so they switch gears. They search for Oscar's social media accounts. There's not much. What is he hiding? There must be something. Everyone is hiding something.

This is why being a private investigator suits them. They are in their element in these moments. All alone and in control.

It might be a good idea to do something that will remind Abby of what's at stake if she loses her focus. Even from the distance they are kept at, Sunny can feel her focus beginning to evaporate, like a shapeless cloud. Sunny is terrified that it will disappear altogether. Which is why they need to step in. When they found Abby, she was a broken shell. She had no purpose. No direction.

They gave those things to her. Put her on the path of retribution. They started by dangling a carrot in the form of an anonymous email. It read, 'Do you want to know more about your father. If so, I can

LITTLE FOXES

help you.' Abby took the bait. Sunny responded with some info about his life and some vague details about his death. They decided that the whole truth might be too much for Abby to handle. After that, the dialogue was open. They didn't even need to bring up the subject of Lee Conrad. She brought it up first, and from then on, it's been a subject of mutual obsession. But Abby gets easily distracted.

They need to send a message that will force Abby to come crawling back to them once more.

Chapter 14

The vase hits the wall beyond his head with a loud crash. Mark Davis looks at his wife. Her face is red and puffy and her body shakes with anger. Her muscles are coiled and tense, like a snake ready to strike. "You. Don't. Love. Me. Anymore." She pauses between each word, taking time to spell it out and let it sink in, as if he is incapable of understanding.

He rubs his temples.

"You're not going to say anything because you can't, because it's true. You clearly aren't attracted to me, and you don't love me anymore." She crosses her arms across her chest, as if she's ashamed of her body. He doesn't understand why. He has seen her naked more times than he can count at this point and, although it has changed a little over the years, it is still mostly the same.

He runs to her and tries to hug her, but she backs away, sitting down in a chair at the kitchen table. She keeps her arms defensively wrapped around herself. "I just don't understand why you don't ever want to be with me."

LITTLE FOXES

He kneels on the floor in front of her. "I'm so sorry. I don't know why either. I wish that I could tell you. I wish that I could make it work, but I can't. I'm just always so tired and stressed from work. He pulls at his hair, frustrated at himself, and lets the tears fall freely from his eyes.

It takes a moment, but she eventually unclasps her hands, and they find his face, wiping the tears away. He scoots towards her, wrapping his arms around the backs of her legs and laying his head down in her lap. She strokes his hair, soothing his pain. He lies and whispers that he will make it up to her another day, when he's feeling better. Deep inside, he feels the anxiety building, churning the acid in the pit of his stomach.

Chapter 15

Abby peeks her head around the corner. Straining her neck, she is trying to make sense of the myriad of smells emanating from the pots and pans. Oscar, upon turning and catching her, sighs and shakes his head. "Tsk, tsk tsk", he scolds. "I thought I told you, no ruining the surprise." He pulls a glass from a shelf and then grabs a large green bottle from a bucket of ice on the counter.

"Isn't that for the meal," asks Abby, raising an eyebrow at him.

"It was", he says, untwisting the wire around the top of the bottle and then pulling out the cork with a loud pop. "But I'm running out of ideas on how to keep you occupied while I finish cooking." He pours her a glass and hands it to her, raising one eyebrow as he does so, and then the other, then both, in a wave motion.

She laughs and takes the glass of champagne. "Well, I suppose alcohol is a step in the right direction," she says, retreating to the living room where she has been banished to occupy herself. She plops down on the large leather sofa with an exaggerated sigh. A moment later she can hear Oscar singing 'dancing queen' to himself from the kitchen. She smiles. He is almost absurdly cute. It is driving Abby crazy. She needs to find something to dislike about this guy.

Setting her glass down on a coaster, she starts looking at the other items on the coffee table, which is just a couple of cooking magazines. She rolls her eyes and then stands, peering around the corner to make sure Oscar isn't looking. She walks nonchalantly around the room, looking at the shelves and under objects for hidden secrets.

She flips through a stack of mail that's laying on an end table. It's mostly credit card bills. Maybe he has bad credit? Who doesn't these days, though, she thinks. She is actually defending him against herself. She's gonna need more than minor credit card debt to talk herself out of this one. She stops at a handwritten envelope. The return address is for a place called Algrove Correctional Wellness facility. The name doesn't sound familiar to her.

She looks up and a photo catches her eye, tucked in a corner of a cluttered shelf. She re-stacks the mail as it was before and then walks to the shelf, picking up the photo to get a closer look at it. It is of a young boy, maybe four or five years old. He is sitting at a table with a cupcake in front of him. Chocolate is smeared all over his face. A woman sits beside him with her arm around him. Her other hand is holding a handkerchief and presumably trying, without much success, to wipe the mess from his chubby cheeks. Something about the mischievous look on the boy's face convinces her that it must be Oscar. There is something about the eyes too, the boy's and the woman's, which are very similar to one another. She is definitely related to him, probably his mother, based on the age difference.

"Are you ready for the best meal you've ever had in your life," Oscar calls out, rapidly approaching from the kitchen. Abby hurriedly puts down the photo and returns to the couch, smiling up at him as he enters. He is gracefully holding a large metal tray, like it's nothing. He sets the tray down on the coffee table in front of her and then pulls off the metal lid, with a dramatic flourish.

Abby skeptically eyes the food on the plate in front of her. It's a sandwich.

"Try it," says Oscar.

Abby lifts the sandwich to her mouth and takes a tentative bite. The sweet juice explodes in her mouth, mixing with a warm sticky texture which has a distinctively nutty flavor. "It's P, B and J", she exclaims, delighted.

"It is homemade roasted cashew butter with blueberry preserves on a fresh baked soft butter croissant."

"That's the same exact thing I just said," she says, smiling. "Is this why you randomly asked if I have a nut allergy the other day?"

LITTLE FOXES

He blushes slightly, becoming even more attractive, if that's possible. "Yes", he replies.

"This is so good," she says, taking another bite. "I think even if I was allergic, I would still risk dying to eat this."

"Oh, I still would've made it either way. I would've just kept an epi-pen on deck while you ate it." As he says this, he reaches over, and wipes preserves from the corner of her mouth.

After the meal, which Abby practically inhales, they snuggle on the couch, watching old sitcoms on TV.

"You know, this date reminds me of lazy afternoons when I was young," says Abby dreamily, while sipping on her wine. "That was back when my parents were still together. Sometimes we would all sit in front of the TV and watch re-runs of Happy Days and other times we would go to this creek by my house to swim. My mom would pack sandwiches. She always packed me P, B and J because it was my favorite. I don't think I've had one since…" Abby trails off.

There is a long silence and Abby starts to think that Oscar hasn't heard her, but then, he grabs her hand and gives it a gentle squeeze. "I'm very sorry if I've brought up painful memories for you," he says quietly. "I know how difficult it is to have parents who…disappoint you."

LITTLE FOXES

Abby breathes a sigh of relief. He thinks she meant that her parents are divorced. He doesn't know about the other thing. Of course he doesn't, how could he? She reassures herself.

Abby turns to look at Oscar and catches him looking at the photo that she had examined earlier. He corrects himself instantly, though, and smiles at her amiably. She smiles back, "I think we need more alcohol," she says, finishing off the rest of her glass. He starts to move, but she puts her hand up. "You stay there and keep the seat warm. I'll get it."

As Abby walks into the kitchen, she turns back to look at him. That woman has got to be his mother, she thinks. I can't believe I'm falling for someone who's even more of a closed book than I am. She thinks again about the story she told him. It's been a long time since she has felt comfortable enough to share anything about her childhood with anyone. Even stories from before what happened are sealed up tightly in a vault that she likes to think is impenetrable. This guy could be my undoing, she thinks, but she still doesn't want to stop.

Chapter 16

He watches the girls go from store to store. They are not buying anything but looking at everything. He follows them into the craft connection. He stays close to the walls, always looking at something…holding something…blending in. He picks up an iron from a shelf and pretends to inspect it. He can see the youngest girl's reflection in the shiny steel. He watches as she picks up a piece of fabric and lifts it to her sister's face, sharing the softness. What else do they share? A little bit later, they leave the store. He follows them out.

He has to duck into an exit corridor when a young man suddenly stops the girls, handing them a microphone and holding up a large camcorder. The red headed one snatches the microphone first, greedily thrusting herself in front of the camera for attention. The dark-haired girl copies the gestures of her friend but doesn't take the microphone. The two blondes stand behind them modestly. The boy takes back the microphone and gives it to the older blonde. She takes it tentatively as the red head scowls at her. Her little sister remains at her side, sheepishly clutching her arm. Then the boy with the camera says something that makes the two sisters laugh together. They are radiant.

LITTLE FOXES

All of a sudden, a large crowd walks in front of the corridor, obscuring his view of the girls. When it clears, they are gone. He walks with renewed purpose towards the food court, assuming that they were headed there. It is bustling with people, and he has to take a turn around the perimeter before catching sight of them. He is momentarily stunned by how close they are to him.

 The older blonde looks directly at him, and he realizes he is standing and staring. Out in the open. He glides backwards, trying to blend into a line that is forming near him so he can resume looking.

He doesn't even register that the red head has left the table until she is there, standing in front of him but not too close. She yells something. He doesn't hear her. It's like his brain is in a fog. He is jolted out of it when she yells, "PERVERT!" at him. He looks around for the first time and realizes that people are starting to look over. To look at him.

He turns and makes for the closest exit. He can't afford to be seen, but he also can't help looking back, one last time. The two sisters stand looking back at him, holding hands. He knows in that moment that he will come back for them.

Chapter 17

Montgomery County Police Station –

"I saw those girls bein taken—the ones in them news reports."

Officer Mark Davis looks at the long- haired young man sitting in front of him. The alcohol and weed waft from his clothes and breath like a raincloud, hovering over the table they are seated at. Davis is new to the missing person's department and the hunt for these two missing girls has been both extensive and relentless.

Many families in the region live in neighborhoods just like the Fox's, including Davis's. They shoo their kids out the door in the morning and catch up with them at suppertime. This is suburbia at its finest. It's supposed to be safe. That's why everyone in the department has taken this case to heart.

There is a sizable reward for any information resulting in a lead into their disappearance. As a newbie, it's Davis's job to sift through the countless witness testimony and sort through the riffraff. This drifter seems like a prime example of the latter.

LITTLE FOXES

He is currently droning on about a young man, possibly a teenager, interviewing the girls at the mall. This is common knowledge. It was reported on the news. It's a thread that the police department pulled early on in the case, but it turned out to be nothing of importance. It was, in fact, a teen interviewing them for a local school news story-something about Easter at the mall. The police had already interrogated the boy and cleared him of any involvement.

Davis yawns. He's been working for twelve hours straight, and this punk's testimony is the same as all the others that he has heard a million times at this point.

"As I were leaving, though, I did see them get into a car. They were with a man; he had a limp."

Davis sits up and looks the young man squarely in the eyes. Several witnesses have spoken about a man "watching" the girls at the mall, but no one has mentioned a limp. Davis looks down at the sheets of paper in front of him. "You go by Greg?"

The young man winces, almost imperceptibly. "I go by my middle name, Lee…Greg's my Daddy's name."

"Okay, Lee, can you tell me the color of the car?"

Lee shifts a little. "Black…wait maybe brown…or navy." He laughs a little awkwardly. "Guess I didn't really take much notice."

LITTLE FOXES

"Okay, what about the man? Height, age, build…anything that could help us?"

"I suppose he was in his thirties or forties, white…walked with a limp."

Davis sighs and rubs his temples. He needs to get some sleep. This doesn't match any of the other descriptions of the mysterious man seen looking at the girls and he's becoming convinced that this stoner is just wasting his time—trying to get the reward money for more drugs.

"Alright Mr. Conrad, Can you take a look over this statement and then sign there at the bottom for me? After that, you can go ahead and head on home. Thank you for your time."

Lee Conrad signs the paper with a jagged, almost childlike signature. "I sure do hope you find them girls", he says, "They are far too innocent to endure the evils of this world."

Chapter 18

There is a man staring at their table. Michelle notices him first. He is standing near the restrooms and just…staring. She would swear too that she had seen the same man at some of the other stores they've shopped in. Is he following them?

"Is that guy looking at us," she asks aloud.

His dirty clothes and ragged appearance make him seem older at first- like a farmer- but then she registers his face. He is in his early twenties, maybe even late teens, with shoulder-length brown, side-swept hair. His eyes are piercing, yet strangely distant, like he's in a trance. His expression is angry and animalistic.

Michelle barely remembers Julie leaving the table, but soon she is a few feet away from him and yelling "PERVERT!", loudly enough for most people to hear. This seems to jolt the man back to consciousness and he walks away.

He turns, however, to look back one last time before disappearing out of sight. Laura grabs a hold of Michelle's hand. Normally, Michelle would be embarrassed by this public display of childlike affection in front of her other friends. But there is something about the way that man looked at them that disturbs her to her core, and she holds on, not wanting to let go.

Chapter 19

The girls leave the mall shortly after the food court. Michelle is relieved. She's been a bit jumpy since the incident with that creepy guy and she just wants to go home. She knows that Laura feels the same because she hasn't stopped clenching her hand tightly, with a surprising grip for such a small girl.

They part ways in the parking lot. Julie and Dawn live in the opposite direction to Michelle and Laura. Michelle drops Laura's hand only to wave at her two friends, with both arms, as they disappear into the horizon.

"OOWWWW!" Laura suddenly screams in pain. Michelle immediately turns and sees her sister on the ground, holding onto her leg. A man is standing hunched over her, as if trying to help.

Michelle runs to her sister and kneels beside her. There is a large bruise on the side of her leg. It is already starting to turn a reddish-purple color. "He kicked me," Laura shrieks when the man tries to touch her leg.

When Michelle turns to look at the man her stomach turns. It is the staring guy from earlier. "Wh…What did you do to her," she asks.

LITTLE FOXES

She feels shocked and confused. Tears begin to sting in the corners of her eyes, making it difficult to see clearly.

"Sorry," he says. "I was just walkin and not payin attention…and I musta accidentally kicked her. It's all my fault. I shouldn'ta worn my work boots. They can pack a pretty big punch." He laughs as he says the last part, although Michelle is not sure why. She looks down at his boots. They are brown and caked in mud.

Michelle grabs Laura's arm and helps her to her feet, although, it's apparent after a couple of attempted steps that she is in a lot of pain and probably unable to walk by herself. Michelle can feel the panic rising inside her. What should she do?

"I don't think she's gonna make it," says the man. "Tell you what. I just feel awful bout this. Why don't I give you a ride home in my van?" He points to a white van not too far away. Laura could probably make it there, with help, but there is something unsettling about the man. Michelle feels uneasy about accepting a ride from him.

Her unease must show on her face because the man smiles, softening his face a little. "I can see that you're a smart girl. Do you know your home phone number by heart?"

Michelle nods warily.

"Good. Good girl. The way I see it, your sister needs your help, so how bout this? The nearest payphone to where we are now is over that way." He points to the right. "It's outside that sporting goods shop in the mall. How about I drive you's over there? Then you can call home and have your parents come git ya. It would just make me feel so much better bout all this."

Michelle wavers. She looks at the vast expanse between where they are and where he pointed out the payphone location. It seems like an unattainable goal, with Laura in her condition.

She nods, trying not to appear as scared as she is. "Just to the payphone."

"Just to the payphone," he agrees.

Chapter 20

Mark Davis tucks in his shirt and secures the badge to his belt. He looks at himself in the mirror. The bags under his eyes are dark and severely contrast with his pale, staunch face. He opens the medicine cabinet. This is the guest bathroom, so it's pretty bare. There is only a bottle of aspirin and some eye drops. He uses the drops, but they don't help much. The desperate look of a man who is in the doghouse remains. He contemplates sneaking into the master bedroom to get to his wife's makeup, specifically her concealer, but decides against it. It's best not to start another argument.

Downstairs, he sips his orange juice and looks at the wedding photo of him and his wife, hanging on the wall of their kitchen. They looked happy. They were, right? He can't even remember. It feels to him now like it was a lifetime ago. He has failed her so much since then. On that day, he wrapped her in his arms and told her they could conquer the world together…and he meant it. Every day since then, though, he's been losing his grip on that feeling and now…well now he just feels nothing about his marriage, except a cold numbness coursing through his veins.

LITTLE FOXES

He finishes his juice, rinses his glass, and places it carefully back in the kitchen cabinet. Then, he quietly slips out the front door, locking it behind him. The house feels foreign to him now, almost as if it was never his at all.

At work he sits at his desk. He transferred to the cold case unit after helping to solve several missing persons and even homicide cases throughout the course of his long career. Now, he mostly files paperwork and performs routine follow-ups for cases that may never be solved.

He is not ungrateful for the path his career has taken. He is a well-respected detective. He's come a long way since his newbie days on the force. Things don't work the way they do in the movies. In real life, cases are solved through slow, meticulous- often clerical- work. He has learned that cases are often solved at a desk, rather than in the field and sometimes, even when there is a trial and a verdict, closure can be difficult to achieve.

These lessons eventually drew him to cold cases. Wouldn't it be the greatest feeling to solve something unsolvable?

Davis flips through his intake of new cold cases, taking notes on each one. The name on one of the files stops him in his tracks. "Fox." He says it out loud, but to himself, as if it's a question. The name sounds so familiar to him and after a few moments, it clicks in his memory.

LITTLE FOXES

He opens a folder on his desktop labelled unsolved MP's. This is his file full of the unsolved missing persons cases which have haunted him throughout the years.

He clicks through, until he finds what he's looking for. He worked this case, along with many other officers, almost twenty years ago. Two young girls went missing at a local mall. This case actually changed the small neighborhood that he still lives in. Parents are stricter on their children and people trust each other a little less.

Later, Davis looks through the seemingly endless rows of boxes for the correct case number. Finally, he finds it. Upon pulling the first one out, he can see that there are at least twenty boxes with the same number. "I guess it's gonna be a long one," he says to himself as he starts pulling out boxes.

Over the next week, Davis scours through the boxes, searching for something…anything that stands out. As he is reading through a police summary, another piece of paper falls out from the middle of the pages. It's a witness summary from the mall on the day the girls disappeared that was somehow hidden away here all these years.

He immediately recognizes the scratchy, straightforward slant of his own handwriting. At first, it seems like a run of the mill statement from that day. The witness, eighteen-year-old Gregory, Lee, Conrad, describes seeing the young high school boy who was interviewing the girls. But then, at the end, there is a note that makes Davis's heart run cold.

Witness claims to have seen girls getting into a car with a thirty something year old white male- with a limp. Upon further questioning, witness could not further describe the man or the vehicle.

Davis stares at the words. He can't believe he didn't follow up on this tip. What was he thinking? The experience-honed alarm bells in his head are ringing off the hook. He needs to investigate this mystery man with a limp further. He needs to make this right.

Davis starts putting out feelers among the department for any information matching the description of the man he is looking for and a couple of weeks later, it pays off. He gets a phone call while sitting at his desk.

"Detective Davis."

"Yes, hello, this is detective Phillips, from over here in sex crimes. I heard you might be looking for a white male with a limp who might be involved in child abduction?"

Davis's ears perk up. "Yes, that's correct." He feels a familiar tightening in his stomach. It's his body's response to eminent, life changing information.

LITTLE FOXES

"Well, I'm glad I found ya, then. I think I know your man. The name is Roy Miller and he's as nasty as they come. He's got a hip injury. Makes the majority of his money through drugs and a child sex trafficking ring. He's currently serving a forty-year sentence for murdering his wife and son. He's about as evil as they come."

Davis is rapidly taking notes. "Can you tell me if he's ever been known to work out of the Allen County area. Turner Hill in particular?"

"Hold on a sec." There is a brief pause. "Yes actually, he's been spotted and picked up by police several times at the Turner Hill mall."

"Thank you. It is much appreciated," says Davis.

"No problem," says Detective Phillips. "I sure hope you can pin it on this fucker. He deserves a fate worse than death, as far as I'm concerned."

Davis's breath hitches in his lungs. This is it; he thinks. I'm going to need to speak to Lee Conrad again.

Chapter 21

Abby scrolls absentmindedly through her Instagram feed. She stops on one of her mother's posts. It's a photo of her mother with her arm placed firmly around Abby's waist. She is smiling overtly at the camera, while Abby looks uncomfortable at best. The caption reads…when someone asks where you came from, the answer is your mother.

Abby rolls her eyes. She zooms in on her own face, critiquing every line and wrinkle. Something she does often. She follows it up by zooming in on her mother's face. She holds it on her expression, trying to decipher every aspect of it. She is smiling, but her eyes tell a different story. Is it disappointment, resentment, jealousy…sadness? Abby zooms out abruptly and drops the phone down on the bed beside her. She picks up her laptop and stares at the screen in front of her.

She decided as soon as she woke up that today was a 'work from your bed' kind of day, but she can't seem to focus. Maybe it's actually a 'get nothing done at all' kind of day.

LITTLE FOXES

Just then, the doorbell rings. Abby trudges begrudgingly from the bedroom, clad in pajamas and slippers. She stands on her tiptoes and looks through the peephole. Oscar is standing there. He is holding a large brown takeout bag and looking around indecisively. Abby smiles and opens the door.

"Well, this is a surprise!"

Oscar looks relieved to see her. "Sorry, I thought it'd be cute and romantic to bring you food on a whim, but then I got here and realized you might be busy or not even home and it started to feel like a stupid idea."

She grabs his arm and pulls him into the apartment. "Never doubt your first instinct", she says, kissing him and forcing him to drop the bag of food and pick her up instead.

A little later, they sit in her bed together eating cold Chinese food.

"You were so cute in your pj's and pink fuzzy slippers," says Oscar, while delicately stroking her bare skin. I was kind of worried you'd be mad at me, though, for just showing up unannounced."

"Why did you decide to come?"

He scrunches up his face a little. "I don't know. Just kind of felt like seeing you."

LITTLE FOXES

Abby lays her head on his chest. His chest hair scratches her face, but it's kind of comforting. She doesn't know what to say. A million thoughts race through her head. She can't tell him that she would never intentionally scare him away by being angry at him. He will leave her eventually, when he discovers what type of person she is. But even though she's not worthy of him, right now she thinks she might need him. She is becoming more and more dependent on his reassuring presence. This is going to be difficult when she ruins everything. She can't say any of that, though, so she says nothing, drifting off to sleep instead.

Chapter 22

The smell of mold burns in her nostrils. Mold and something else…sweat. She moves her face a little to the side. Prickly fibers and bits of dirt and crumbs scrape against her cheek. The throbbing pain returns to her all at once, like an avalanche. She wants to rub her head, where it hurts the most, but she can't. She realizes that her arms are tied behind her back.

Deafening confusion pulses through her. She lifts her head as much as she can and looks around her. She can tell that she is in the back of a van. There are no windows, only darkness. She can hardly see around her, but she can make out a shape in the corner.

Memories come rushing back to fill in the gaps of her mind. The shape is one of those swivel chairs they use in computer lab. Sometimes the boys in class will try to wheel through the aisles and get back to their computer before the teacher notices. Pure bliss shines on their faces when they make it. She has always secretly wished she had the guts to try it, so she could feel that feeling- just once.

LITTLE FOXES

As she looks at the chair, exhaustion pushing down her eyelids, it begins to move. It swivels around toward her with a slow creak and then it slides closer and closer. When it is about half a foot away, she can start to make out two brown work boots, caked with mud.

Panic sets in. She screams as loudly as she can, desperately hoping someone will hear her. Arms grab a hold of her hair, pulling roughly, and something that smells even worse than the dirty carpet is shoved down her throat, violently cutting off her air. She chokes and cries, sucking air in rapidly through her nose and then…she loses consciousness again.

Chapter 23

Abby sits upright with a start. She wipes the tears from her face. That dream again.

She looks over to her side and is surprised to see an empty space with the covers pushed back in a messy heap. She splashes water on her face in the bathroom then pulls on a robe and wanders out into the living room and kitchen area. Empty. Then, she checks the guest bathroom. Also empty. Did he leave? Either that, or…she looks at the door to her office. It is slightly ajar and there is a soft glow emanating through the crack.

Abby tentatively opens the door. Her desk lamp is on, but other than that, the room is empty. She walks towards the closet and throws open the door. Her coats are still there, hiding her secrets. She is about to pull them apart when she hears the front door open. She exits the room to find Oscar, trying to close the door as quietly as he can.

"Where did you go," she asks, unable to keep the paranoia out of her voice.

LITTLE FOXES

He jumps and turns to look at her. His face is flushed. Cold or embarrassment? "I…I got a phone call," he stammers, holding up his cell phone as if it's existence in his hand explains everything. "I didn't want to wake you up, so I went outside. God, it's cold out there," he says, rubbing his hands together and answering her silent accusations.

She stares him down, trying to read his mind. She wants to trust him, but she has a nagging feeling that he knows more than he is letting on.

"I grabbed your mail while I was out there," he says. His expression is cheerful as he holds out a stack of envelopes and flyers, like it's a normal thing to do.

She takes the mail from his hand begrudgingly.

"Anyway, my boss is the one who called me. They need me at the restaurant, so…I'm gonna go get my stuff together."

He pauses while saying it, as if expecting her to interject with passionate tears and a bleeding heart.

She remains silent.

He walks past her to the bedroom and then back out again. She sits at her kitchen table absentmindedly opening the mail in front of her and trying to look nonchalant. She doesn't know what to say, not until she knows what he knows. He walks towards her and kisses her awkwardly. She lets him but doesn't give anything back.

Once he is gone, her mind races to come up with a plan. She will need to get some dirt on him, to use as leverage, just in case.

With a plan beginning to form in her mind, she eases up a bit. She looks down at the envelope in front of her. Magazine letters have been cut out and glued to the front of the envelope, spelling out Abby. There is nothing else. No return address or even so much as her apartment number. That's odd, she thinks as she rips it open.

She unfolds the piece of paper on the inside. There are two words spelled out, once again with magazine letters, in the middle of the page. I KNOW. Those two words shake Abby to her core.

Chapter 24

"Uuumm, shoulder length, and like an ugly brown." Julie and Dawn sit at a desk, speaking to a police officer.

"Hey," says Dawn. Her face is streaked with tears.

"Oh shut up, I just meant that his hair was like an ugly brown color, not yours stupid."

"Like this?" The officer turns his sketchbook towards them. The girls strain their necks to see it over the desk, which is littered with file folders and coffee cups and a half-eaten sandwich.

"He had a fatter nose," says Julie.

"Yeah, and his hair was kind of side-swept in the front," says Dawn.

"And you're sure this man was looking at you all?"

"He was staring like a Pervert, which is why I called him one. Are you calling us liars," Julie asks.

The officer ignores her outburst and looks over at Dawn for confirmation.

LITTLE FOXES

"He was staring a lot, sir. I actually thought that we should tell an adult or something, but then Julie scared him away and we left. I just didn't think that anything would happen. Oh god…" she breaks off, sobbing.

Julie reaches over and embraces Dawn, the two of them stay that way, huddled and crying together.

Chapter 25

Detective Davis tries to recall the man sitting before him, but twenty years- ten spent in prison- have wearied away at his features. He is fairly certain, though, that Lee remembered him instantly, since the first words out of his mouth were, "I know why you're here. You're here about those two missing kids."

Now the two of them sit, looking at one another. Davis, trying to reconcile the past with the man sitting before him and Lee, with a sly grin on his face.

Davis has mentally prepared himself for a tough-shelled stoner, like the young man who first came to him all those years ago. He had thought very carefully about how to start this conversation, but all his planning went right out of his head with Lee's first words. He is scrambling to collect his thoughts, trying to think of a way to re-gain control of the situation, when, completely un-provoked, Lee begins to talk.

"My mom died when I was just a kid. My daddy was a terrible drunk. He was mean. He used to yell, throw things. Sometimes he would

LITTLE FOXES

grab me by the neck and throw me." Lee chuckles a little at his own words and then looks up at Davis, as if for approval.

Davis sits back in his seat, crossing his arms and settling in. He's interested.

Lee continues, "One day, when I was around ten, we all piled into the truck to go to the store. It was winter and there was snow on the ground and black ice on the roads. I had wanted to play outside, there was this neighbor girl. We used to play together in the snow. She had the whitest hair. Her cheeks used to get all rosy in the cold." Lee pauses for a moment, seemingly lost in thought, but then he continues. "But pop wouldn't let me, said Mom needed groceries and I had to help her. He was already falling over drunk, but he grabbed another beer from the fridge on the way out, stuck it between his legs while he drove. I was too upset about missing play time to care about anything else…not that I coulda done anything to stop it anyway."

He pauses again. Looking down at his feet. Davis remains quiet, letting him have a moment.

"Have you ever seen a dead person?"

Davis is taken aback. He has, in fact, over the course of his long career, seen several dead bodies. Both in photos and in real life. It is something that always sticks with you.

LITTLE FOXES

Lee continues, without letting him respond. "At first, when we hit the ice and started sliding around all over the place, I remember thinking it was fun, like a crazy roller coaster ride, but then…we crashed. I woke up in the worst pain I've ever been in, the doctor's said I hit my head off the dashboard, but at least I was alive…unlike her.

My mom was half-out of the car. Broke through the windshield. There was glass everywhere and it was so cold. Her face was all bloody and her eyes were open, just staring. Good old Pop was fine of course, not a scratch on im. He was passed out, though. I screamed and screamed for him to wake up, but he just slept right through the whole damn thing."

Davis can sense Lee's anger rising. He remembers back to their first interview when he had insisted on not being called Gregory. That's my daddy's name, he had said. "That must've been tough for you to go through all that."

Lee sighs and puts his head in his hands. "It was, but then, of course it just kept getting worse. I was taken away from him- drunk as he was- and put in foster home after foster home. Each one is worse than the one before. Like they were punishing me for not being the perfect well-behaved child."

LITTLE FOXES

"And how could they expect you to be with the lousy role model you had growing up," asks Davis, trying to gain some common ground.

Lee nods in approval. "Yeah, and now I'm in here. The world was shitty to me, and I became a shitty person. Circle of life, I guess." For a moment his face takes on a hard, sinister look that freezes Davis's blood in his veins, but then it disappears, replaced by a smile.

"But nuff about me, I know you're here about those girls. The two that disappeared all them years ago."

"Now, how do you know that" asks Davis, returning his smile.

Lee looks into Davis's eyes, searching for something. After a while he says, "I figured one day you guys'd want to follow up with me about what I told you about the man, with the limp."

"Yes", says Davis. He pulls a photo from a folder and places it in front of Lee. "Is this the man you saw leaving from the mall with the two Fox girls that day?"

The corners of Lee's mouth lift a little in a twitching motion. "You know, I think it just might be."

"And, just for the record, can you explain again how you saw them leaving together?"

LITTLE FOXES

"I saw him leading them right out the front doors, into the parking lot. He had his hand on the back of the older girl's neck, and she was pulling the younger one along with her. I think the younger one was crying. That's what caught my attention in the first place."

"Did you see them enter a vehicle together?"

"Not sure. I kinda lost sight of em."

Davis rubs his chin, thinking over Lee's words. "Okay, well Lee, I think I've taken up enough of your time for one day," he says, standing and pushing a button on the wall of the room.

"No bother, I've got nothing but time in here. "Until next time," he says as a prison guard escorts him from the room.

On the drive home, Davis thinks about the exchange. Something doesn't quite seem right. Why did his story change?

Chapter 26

She can hear the screaming from the living room below. It emanates through the walls of the little house. Every word is a stab in her gut.

"Are you telling me I can't come home and have a drink", her stepfather's voice booms out. "What do you want me to do, sit here with nothing to do, but watch TV and think about all the things that happened. I can't even look at her anymore. I just…can't take this pressure!"

A moment later the front door slams and her mother's sobbing begins.

She reaches for the discman that is sitting on her bedside table. It was a Christmas gift last year. She had been so excited. She had walked around for a week, singing songs that no one else could hear at the top of her lungs. Now, she pulls the headphones over her ears, she changes it to the last track – Perfect by Simple Plan- and sets it on repeat, turning the volume up all the way and pulling the covers up over her face.

She pulls a safety pin from her pocket and plunges it deep into the fatty part of her thumb. She continues pushing it down, as far as she can. When the pain sets in, it washes over her. She can't use a knife or a razor blade because her mother inspects her constantly these days, looking at her with those accusing eyes that seem to ask, why are you doing this to me? This way it doesn't leave much of a mark, but it still hurts just enough to momentarily replace the sadness.

Chapter 27

Abby jolts awake. Her hand moves to the scar on her arm. Then, she rubs the tips of her fingers, remembering the pain. She pulls up her pant leg and touches the thin, red lines that mark the back of her leg. The one's she put there later, after she moved out of her mom's house. She rubs her temples wearily. She's been dreaming a lot about it lately.

She grabs her phone and scrolls through her social media accounts. She searches for Oscar. There's nothing on Facebook or twitter. There is an old Instagram with one old photo of a homemade pizza and a glass of wine. She thinks back to the letter that she found in his apartment and opens a new internet search, typing in 'Algrove Correctional Wellness Facility'. She clicks on a website link, which takes her to an information page. It reads; 'Algrove Correctional Wellness Facility is a medium security level facility for females. Our mission is to create a safe environment for offender management and supervision in our facilities and communities- while holding offenders accountable and promoting their rehabilitation'.

Offender management? Why's he getting mail from a low-key prison, Abby thinks to herself.

LITTLE FOXES

She goes back to the Instagram photo. She looks at all the comments. There are a lot of "oooo's" and "looks yummy" and one "you can cook for me anytime", from a particularly done up- highly filtered- barely clothed, young woman, which makes Abby angrier than she expected. She starts clicking on each person who commented, checking out their pages one by one. A lot of them are set to private. She starts to scroll through the photos of a fifty-something year old woman's page absentmindedly, but then stops dead in her tracks. There is a photo of this woman with Oscar. They are half-hugging, and he is holding up a diploma from the culinary institute of Delaware. He looks so young and happy.

The comments are where Abby hits pay-dirt, though. There is one from Oscar; "Thanks for being there for me when no one else could."

The woman replied back; "Of course. Have you visited your mom at ACWF lately? She misses you a lot."

ACWF- Algrove Correctional Wellness Facility- the prisoner he receives mail from is his mom.

Chapter 28

Detective Davis sits at an outside restaurant table, enjoying the nice weather. A short time later, a man with salt and pepper hair and intense eyes walks up to the table and introduces himself as detective Chris Phillips.

"Thanks for meeting with me", says Davis. "I wanted to find out more about Roy Miller."

"Sure, I'm pretty much an expert. What do you want to know?"

"Well, Everything."

Phillips calls over the waitress and orders some appetizers and a beer. "We're gonna be here a while," he says to Davis after ordering.

An hour and a half later, Davis is once again taking notes and trying to keep up as Phillips paints a picture of evil incarnate. "I spoke to one woman who grew up near him. She said that he had raped her multiple times as a teenager and that he would lure other teens to his house in Maryland by having what he called 'sex parties', which were stocked with alcohol and drugs. He had a crew and, with a lot of hard questioning, many of the men who worked for him admitted that they had been initiated as teenagers and intimidated into engaging in sex acts. At these parties, he would drug young people and then 'share' them with his clients."

"Why did he shoot his wife and son," asks Davis.

"Not sure. He would never say, but there was a rumor that they could've implicated him in a murder."

"Have you ever heard of Lee Conrad?"

"Hmmm," Phillips rubs his chin. "Name definitely sounds familiar."

"He's currently serving time in Delaware for sex crimes involving children. Given your area of expertise, I thought you might know something about it."

Something clicks in Philip's expression. "Conrad, yeah, I'm pretty sure he was picked up for raping multiple girls. Young girls. The one they had the most evidence for was fourteen or fifteen, I think. He would often abduct them in his van and drive out to a remote location in the woods where no one could hear them scream. The last time, though, he got cocky. Brought her back to his house. The girlfriend called the police."

Davis shivers. "I'm not sure yet, but I think he might be connected somehow to this. He was at the mall when the girls were abducted.

LITTLE FOXES

He came forward as a witness when he was nineteen. Do you think it's possible that he and Miller knew each other?"

"It's possible. You know how these scumbags like to stick together. There would've been quite an age difference, but that doesn't mean much, especially given Roy's proclivity for younger men. It also probably would've been easier for a younger man to lure two young girls from the mall, rather than a middle-aged man. It's worth looking into."

Chapter 29

Later, Davis sits at his desk, phone pressed to his ear. He is trying to make an appointment to see Roy Miller in prison, but he has been placed on hold.

He sits, tapping his foot against the floor and thinking. Phillips is fully convinced that Roy Miller is good for this, but the more Davis looks into Lee Conrad, the more the sinking feeling in the pit of his stomach grows. It's true Roy worked that area and that he targeted younger victims, but they always seemed to be in their late teens or early twenties, whereas Lee's known rape victims were as young as eight and no older than fifteen. Michelle Fox was twelve years old, and Laura Fox was ten.

The phone crackles in his ear. "Hello, Detective?"

"Yes, I'm still here," he answers, sitting up and getting ready to take notes.

"I'm sorry, you won't be able to speak to Roy Miller after all."

"Why's that?"

"He passed away recently."

LITTLE FOXES

Davis is stunned. "Can I ask how?"

"Report just says natural causes. He was eighty-two years old."

Chapter 30

She plunges deep into the water, brushing her fingers against the smooth stones at the bottom of the creek bed. When she emerges, she whips around until she spots her father and mother, sitting on a blanket on the shore. Her father's arm is around her mother. They both smile at her and wave. She waves back. This is the happiest she's ever been.

Chapter 31

The buzzing alarm jars Abby awake. She pulls herself reluctantly out of the bed. It's not often her dreams are nice. She didn't want it to end. But even now, as she fills the coffee pot with water, the memory is fading fast, and the coldness of reality is seeping in to fill the hole it leaves behind.

While waiting for the coffee pot to fill, she peruses through the stack of unopened mail on the counter. One letter catches her eye and makes her hair stand on end. It is a plain envelope; her name is spelled out in colorful magazine letters. Just like the last one. She opens it hastily, ripping the envelope. This time a newspaper clipping falls out. It flutters to the floor, like a feather, landing face-up.

Abby recognizes the article instantly. She has a copy of the newspaper it came from packed away in a box under her bed. Something is different about this one, though. There are two words from the article that are circled in red ink. She picks up the paper to get a closer look. The first circled word is I, the second is know. Someone knows about her past and is taunting her. Could it be Oscar?

LITTLE FOXES

Abby contemplates going to the police, but she doesn't trust them. She will call Sunny instead.

Sunny is a private investigator she has hired before. They've never met in person. They always communicate via email. In fact, it was Sunny who first reached out to Abby. They sent her an email, out of the blue, asking if Abby was interested in finding out what had happened to her real father. Abby did want to know. Not all the details, though, just the broad strokes. And Sunny's intel seemed legit. Abby is not even sure if they are a man or a woman, but she does know that no one is better at exposing the truth.

Chapter 32

Detective Davis walks out of the Maryland State Penitentiary. He decided to visit Roy Miller's cellmate. Guys like Roy tend to brag, and he had a hunch that he might've said something about the Fox girls to someone. A hunch that partially paid off.

His cellmate, a tattooed thug doing time for gang violence, said that Roy would talk a lot about the missing girls and how he knew exactly what happened to them. When pressed, though, he would swear up and down that he had nothing to do with their kidnapping, but that he 'probably could tell you where the bodies were buried'.

It wasn't proof that Roy had anything to do with the girls' disappearance, but it was enough to make Davis want to look into this asshole some more.

Around the time of the disappearance, Roy was living in a house that was not too far from the Turner Hill Mall. Davis has already spoken to the elderly woman who lives there now and convinced her to let him check the place out.

Davis's nostrils are affronted with a damp, mildewy smell that often accompanies old, country houses like this one. After inspecting the yard, a tiny plot without much potential for burying two bodies, he has made his way into the house and is walking through the main level. The floorboards creak under his shoes, but nothing strikes him as out of the ordinary. Then, he spots an old looking door that seems to lead somewhere.

"Where does that lead?" He calls to Mrs. Hannigan, the elderly lady, sitting in front of the TV and trying her best to ignore his presence in her house.

"Basement", she answers shortly.

He opens the door and tentatively makes his way down the thin, wooden staircase. He finds a light switch at the bottom and pushes it up. A light in the center of the basement creates a dim, yellow glow casting parts of the large, open room in dingy shadows. Other than the creepy ambiance, it seems to be a fairly typical basement…save for one thing.

Davis's father owned a carpentry business and he had grown up learning the trade and working for him throughout his high school and college years. That's why he can tell immediately that the carpeting in this basement had been added later than the rest by a layman, not a professional. What if Roy Miller had added the carpeting to cover something up?

LITTLE FOXES

Without thinking, Davis grabs a piece of the carpet in the corner of the room and begins to pull. An hour later, he's pulled up most of the carpet and is frantically inspecting the floor underneath. He shines his flashlight on every inch, looking for any sign of evidence on the cement floor underneath.

"What on earth do you think you're doing," a voice screeches out from the basement stairs. Davis turns to see Mrs. Hannigan standing there, hands on her hips, and a very disapproving expression on her face.

"I needed to check the floor," he answers defensively. Then he adds in a softer tone, "Don't worry, I'll pay to have it re-carpeted."

Mrs. Hannigan shakes her head and sighs. "I hope you at least found what you were looking for," she says and then turns, heading glumly back up the stairs.

Davis puts his head in his hands and his emotions wash over him. What is he doing? This whole thing feels like he's being led on a wild goose chase.

Chapter 33

She crawls forward on her hands and knees. She stops when she gets to a box labeled 'photos. She rips off the lid and rummages through the box until she finds the one she's looking for. It's an old photo of a young man. His arm is wrapped tightly around a young woman- her mother- who is holding a baby. She knows in her heart that this is a photo of her and her dad. She strokes the photo lovingly, trying to imagine his voice telling her how much he loves her.

"Lunch is ready…get down here." Her mother calls from downstairs.

She hastily puts the photo back in the box and scrambles out of the attic crawl space. Once downstairs, she sits at the table with her mom, still thinking about her dad. Her mom never talks about her dad, but she has so many questions bubbling up inside her that she can't help it when they start spilling out.

"Where is my dad?"

Her mother glances at her nonchalantly. She looks tired these days. Dark circles encompass her eyes and she's been smoking more and more frequently. Lacie doesn't like it. The smoky smell clings to everything, making her feel like she can't breathe. "He's at work. You know that", her mother responds.

"No," she says, frustrated at not being understood. "My REAL dad."

Her mother looks at her- really looks at her. Her face is full of surprise, but also pain.

She wants to back pedal and say she's sorry, but it's too late for that.

"Jeff is your real dad and if you're going to be so ungrateful, you can go spend the afternoon in your room without lunch." She snatches the plate from in front of her daughter and dumps the contents into the trash can.

Later that evening, she sneaks back to the attic crawl space. It looks like someone cleaned it out. Frantic, she searches, pulling the lids off all the remaining boxes and dumping the contents on the floor, but it's no use. The photo is gone.

Chapter 34

The realization dawns on Abby that she's been standing at her kitchen counter, unmoving for…how long? She takes a sip from the coffee mug that is in her hand, but immediately spits it back out into the mug. It is ice cold. She pours it out in the sink and rinses the mug. Something catches her eye, in the corner of the kitchen counter.

There is a line of countertop skirting about three to four inches high that goes the whole way around the wall. There, just beyond the dry rack, in the corner, there is something sticking out between the wall and the skirting.

Abby pulls on the end of it, trying to free it from the small space. Finally, it comes out, sending her backwards a step. She looks down at it in bewilderment. She holds it up to the light, wondering if it will change, like a hologram. It doesn't, though. The photo remains the same. It is her father, holding her as a baby. It's the same photo that she thought her mother threw away all those years ago. How did it get here?

LITTLE FOXES

A knock at the door brings Abby back to reality. She hastily shoves the photo into her back pocket. When she opens the door, she is greeted by Oscar's wide grin.

"You seemed stressed on the phone, so I snuck some wine from the restaurant." He holds his finger up to his lips. "Sssshhh, don't tell."

Abby is confused. When did she call him? Is this a game? If it is, he isn't going to win this round. She can hold her own at the table with the high rollers. She smiles adoringly and flutters her eyelashes. "Wow, so thoughtful, babe!"

He beams down at her, seemingly genuine. He's good, she'll give him that. She takes the wine bottle and pours two glasses, even though she has no intention of actually drinking hers. She swirls the dark liquid around in the glass, as they sit and watch TV.

Every so often, he says something, and she nods and smiles, pretending to listen, but she can't get her mind off the photo. Who put it there? When she stands to get them more wine, he either doesn't notice or doesn't say anything about the fact that her own glass is still full.

When she returns to the couch, she almost drops the glasses in her hands. Oscar is sitting there, holding the photo of her and her dad. Her hands won't stop shaking. She puts the glasses down on the

LITTLE FOXES

coffee table and tries to steady herself. "Where did you get that," she asks in the sweetest voice she can muster.

Oscar grins. "It fell out of your pocket when you stood up. Is that you as a baby?"

Abby's head is swimming. It feels as though it's full of wine, even though she didn't drink any. What does this mean? How likely is it that the photo just fell out of her back pocket? "You know what, I just remembered, I have some work to get done."

"Well, maybe I can just hang out til you're done. I just drank a glass of wine, and I don't mind just chilling if it means I get to be with you." Oscar grins at her again.

Why is he trying so hard? "Yeah, I just think that I need to be alone, so I can concentrate and all. Don't worry about the wine. I'll get you an uber", she says while simultaneously clicking buttons on her cell phone.

"But I drove here. What about my car?"

He looks a little sad now, so she decides to throw him a bone. "You can come back later and get it." She extends her leg and runs her toe along the side of his jeans.

LITTLE FOXES

He grabs hold of her leg and then starts tickling her. Before she knows what's happening, he's on top of her, tickling her, and she is laughing and out of breath, despite herself.

Abby pushes him off her abruptly and ushers him towards the door. "See how distracting you are." she says, smiling. "Thank you for understanding. I promise I will see you later."

Oscar kisses her tenderly. He strokes her hair away from her face. "I'll see you later," he says with a pointed expression.

"Later," she responds.

Once he's gone, she is overwhelmed with both relief and sadness. She must figure out the mystery of this photo, but first…she walks to the kitchen and grabs the bottle of wine, no need for a glass. She props the photo up on her coffee table in front of her. She drinks and stares at it, giving in to the sadness that has taken hold of her.

Chapter 35

Sunny cuts the article from the worn newspaper page with extreme delicacy. It pains them a little because they know how much it means to Abby, but it's something they must do.

Once it's done, they fold the newspaper back up and place it very carefully in the shoebox, which they push back under the bed.

Abby will be scared when she receives the clipping, terrified even. It should be enough to push her towards action.

Sunny places the clipping in her pocket and sneaks out of the apartment. They leave everything as it was when they arrived. Well, almost everything. On their way out, they take a photo from their pocket and wedge it in between the countertop skirting and the wall in the kitchen. They leave one corner sticking out where it will inevitably be discovered.

Then they leave, locking the door, with their own key. Copying it was the first thing they did when they took Abby on as a client, and it has since come in handy.

LITTLE FOXES

They see a lot of themself in Abby and their heart feels for her. She needs to learn that she can't trust anyone, though. By any means necessary.

Chapter 36

Detective Davis studies the papers spread out all over the table. There are photos of the two girls and of the mall where they disappeared. In the center of the pile is a large blueprint of the mall's layout. Davis tries to set the scene in his mind. Imagining the girls walking from store to store – someone lurking in the shadows, watching them. They make their way to the food court, where he is exposed, the staring man, but is he the same person who took the girls? He must be, right? But Julie scares him away from them…and then what?

Davis's wife enters the dining room with a casserole dish in her hands. When she sees the state of the table, she sighs a heavy sigh, pulling Davis from his concentration. "I'm just going to eat upstairs. I can see that you most likely won't be bothering to come up tonight anyways." There is a biting tone to her voice, but also a faint hint of a hopeful question.

Davis only waves at her in response. There are some cases that take a hold of you deep inside as a detective, and for him, this is one of them. He didn't do enough the first time around, but this time, he will let it wash over him and consume him. Whatever it takes. He is back in his mind's eye and his wife is right, nothing will pull him out of it.

Chapter 37

Davis clocks the slight smile that flutters across Lee's face when he is escorted into the room. Is it possible that he is excited to see him? By the time Lee is seated, however, his expression is once again blank, like he has no idea how or why he is here.

"Hello Lee. How's it goin", Davis asks, keeping the mood light-hearted.

"Well, I'm bored as hell and the food in here is shit," Lee responds. Always the victim.

"That's not what we want to hear," says Davis, playing along. "Maybe I can help you out a little with your commissary…but first, I need some more help with this abduction case. Do you remember it."

Lee seems pleased, but only nods.

"You see, I've run into a bit of a dead end," continues Davis. I searched Roy Miller's old house. There was nothing out of the ordinary, no traces of any blood or bodies being buried there. I also found an interesting file the other day. It seems that Roy had been considered pretty early on in the case, but that he was ruled out

LITTLE FOXES

because he was out of town that weekend. So, I went back to the drawing board. I re-interviewed several of the witnesses that were at the mall that weekend and you know what happened?"

Lee says nothing.

"None of them remembered seeing Roy Miller there. The only person who claims to have seen him there…is you." Davis takes a beat, letting his words sink in before he continues. "So now, I'm stuck between a rock and a hard place because on one hand, the only thread I have left to pull on is you, but on the other side, I heard this story last time I was here about a boy. A boy who was a victim himself. A boy who deserves to get out of this awful place in a few years and become a free man. But…this case is eating away at my insides. I need to know what happened to those girls. Their family needs to know where their bodies are, so they can put them to rest, in peace." Davis wasn't sure if he should add that last part. Pleading to a monster's compassion can be a tricky business. Another man- put away for murdering multiple women- had once told him, "People like me-we don't feel remorse. In its place, you will only find emptiness."

But, as he searches Lee's expression, he thinks he may have struck a nerve somewhere. The muscles in Lee's jaw are strained and held tight, like he's restraining himself from emotion.

LITTLE FOXES

Davis continues to push. "Can you tell me what you think happened?"

He waits for what seems like an eternity for a response. When Lee begins to talk, his voice is low at first, but it gets louder and more confident as he gains momentum. "My opinion, they were probably raped, but maybe they got to be too much of a hassle, you know, complaining too much or whatever, and they were killed for it. Around those parts, their bodies probably would've been burned up, a long time ago.

My cousin, Wes, used to look up to me when he was little. He is a few years younger than me. He used to follow me around everywhere sayin, 'What you doin Lee, can I come with you, Lee?' Then, when he was about thirteen or so, he just up and disappeared. I asked my family what happened to him, but no one gave me a straight answer. I just didn't give it another thought… until he showed back up years later, when he was fifteen. He introduced me to this old man. In his fifties, at least. His name was like, William Beaumont, or something fancy like that." Lee pronounces the name with a posh accent for accentuation. "And get this, Wes introduced him to me as 'his lover'. He had stories of travelling to all sorts of places with him. Paris, Italy, Mexico. That faggot went out and got himself a sugar-daddy, see?"

LITTLE FOXES

Lee pauses, a humorous expression on his face. Davis laughs nervously. It's an uncomfortable high-pitched sound. "Wow, I don't even have the words for that," he says.

Lee laughs too. Then he continues. "I only bring all this up because you're askin me what happened and I tell you, I don't know for sure. I sure as hell didn't kill no one, but Wes came back right before those girls disappeared and he left with that weirdo again a little bit after the police started askin questions. I haven't thought about it until now, but the timing does strike me as odd, you know?"

Davis nods but doesn't reply. He has learned that if he just stays quiet, Lee will continue to offer stories to him. It will be up to Davis to sift through those stories and separate the fact from the fiction.

Lee continues. "And also, now I think of it, he used to brag about all the fancy clothes his sugar-daddy used to buy for him and how girls back then were like…how did he put it?" Lee scratches his bald head. As he does, flakes of dry skin fall to the table in front of him like little flakes of snow. Lee brushes the table off quickly, grunting something incoherent. As he moves his arm, the metal of the handcuff keeping him secured to the table makes a clinking noise which is somewhat jarring in the midst of their conversation.

"A moth to a flame," he finishes his thought. "He said they were drawn to fancy things and I'm pretty sure I remember him talkin about luring some young girls from the mall around that time. Now I think of it, he was probably sharin them with that creepy old fairy friend of his."

Lee places his elbows on the table, hands clasped together, and looks Davis square in the eyes. A look of self-satisfaction covering his features, like a challenge.

Chapter 38

Abby wakes to the smell of bacon and waffles. The scent of the sweet, fried dough and greasy meat tangle together and waft through the apartment, reaching her nose and pulling her awake and out of bed like a magical spell.

When she enters the kitchen, she finds the source of the wizardry. Oscar is there with a smorgasbord of breakfast food everywhere. Every burner of her little-used stove is in use, and he even bends over to pull something out of the oven. When he sees her, he looks startled at first, but then smiles. "Surprise," he says weakly. I was hoping for things to be a little less chaotic before you woke up, but I promise it's going to be amazing once it's done. The best thing you've ever eaten!"

It is the best thing she's ever eaten. The waffles melt in her mouth and the bacon is that perfect combination of crisp and fatty. There are even perfectly fluffy scrambled eggs and homemade croissants. Abby shovels the food into her mouth like It's the first meal she's had in days. Come to think of it, she can't recall what she had to eat the previous day, but she must've eaten something, right?

LITTLE FOXES

Oscar smiles at her from across the table. "Slow down there, speed racer," he says. "I'm very happy that you seem to like it, but I also would be very sad if you choked to death." He puffs out his lower lip and widens his eyes, pantomiming a sad expression.

She sets her fork down and smiles back at him. "Sorry," she says, still chewing. "I'm just really hungry, I guess." Abby eats the rest of her breakfast at a more reasonable pace, but still finishes every last bite and some of what is left on Oscar's plate.

"Okay, I cooked, now you can do the dishes," says Oscar, once she has finally relinquished her plate to him. She looks at the huge pile of dishes taking over the whole sink and spilling over onto the countertops. Oscar laughs at her befuddled expression. "I'm just kidding. What if we work together?"

Abby dries the dishes and puts them away, while Oscar washes and rinses them. Every now and then, he splashes water on her playfully, before handing her a new dish. And she stares at him while drying them, studying his handsome features. Then, when she finishes a dish, she pinches his side saying, "Where's my next dish, huh?"

It's in these moments, she forgets about her suspicions and feels truly happy. When the doorbell rings, however, Abby is quick to abandon her dish drying post, which she was only half-assing anyway. When she opens the door, there is an amazon package sitting on her welcome mat.

"Another amazon package", says Oscar, seeing the box in her hands. "I think you might be keeping them in business."

What does that mean, she thinks. It's comments like that which make it difficult for her to understand him at times. Curiosity gets the better of her, however, and she shrugs his comments away and rips open the box, letting it fall to the floor. Inside is…craft supplies. Markers, glue sticks, scissors, tape. You would think she was a child with a school project coming up. Abby is confused. She doesn't remember ordering these things. She looks around her for the box, thinking that maybe it accidentally got delivered to the wrong apartment. But the box is nowhere to be seen.

"Where is it, where's the box," she asks, looking all around her.

Oscar blinks at her. "I picked it up and threw it away. Didn't you see me?"

"No," she answers. Her voice is tinged with accusation. "Why are you sneaking around throwing away my things? This was obviously delivered to the wrong place."

"I...I'm sorry," he stammers. "I didn't know you needed it. You did just rip it up and throw it all over the floor. I thought I was helping. Plus, I thought you were just getting more supplies for your project."

A strange headache starts to fill up Abby's head with warmth. "What project?"

"You know, the surprise present you've been working on for your mom?"

Abby stares at him blankly. What is this guy's deal? Is he trying to make her seem crazy? She needs to think, but the headache is getting worse, making it impossible. "You know, speaking of that present, I need to work on it, so you should probably go. After all, I don't want to spoil the surprise."

He looks upset. "Really? I thought we were hanging out today."

"Yeah, I know, but I just remembered that I have a ton of stuff to get done and I kind of need to be alone to do it." She flashes him a smile. "But you can come back later tonight if you want."

He still looks sad, but smiles back, weakly. "Alright. I guess I'll see you later, then."

Once he is gone, Abby lays down on her bed. She needs to sleep off this headache so she can think.

Chapter 39

They sit in silence, staring at the wall. Abby's dirty little secret obsession that she so desperately doesn't want him to discover. This new flame in her life is bad news. She is losing her focus. It looks like it will, once again, be up to Sunny to bring her attention back to the important matters at hand.

They stand and very carefully remove one of the photos from the wall. They place the photo in the center of Abby's office desk, where they know she will see it.

At that moment, the cell phone in their pocket vibrates. It's him.

They decide to answer, holding the phone up to their ear tentatively.

"Hello sweets, I was wondering if it'd be okay if I came over later so we can hang out?"

They silently contemplate their choices. This could be an interesting way to drive a wedge between them and they want to see how it will play out.

They muster their best Abby voice, "Sure, can't wait."

LITTLE FOXES

Then, they hang up and leave the room, making sure that the desk lamp is on, shining directly at the photo of young Abby sitting in the middle of the desk.

Chapter 40

Abby takes a wary step forward. She glides forward a little as her blades meet the ice. She almost falls backwards but catches herself on the handrail. Oscar comes up behind her and then gracefully swooshes around to face her. "Hey there, beautiful," he says, making her blush. "Here, take my hand." He holds his gloved hand out to her, and she takes it tentatively.

She tries to hold on to the wall with her other hand for as long as she can, but, eventually, he guides her forward to the point of no return. Abby looks in his eyes and decides to try trusting him. She lets go of the wall and pushes herself forward.

For a few shining moments, she is gliding majestically forward, and it is exhilarating! But then, she notices a turn coming up and loses her nerve, and with it, her balance. She falls to the ground, taking Oscar with her and for a confusing moment, they are a jumble of bulky winter clothing.

Oscar is able to get to his knees quickly and leans over her, concern dripping from his features, as she lays prone on the ice. She can feel the cold on the back of her head. She looks up at the sky. The stars are bright – soothing. Just then, she realizes Oscar is speaking to her.

"Abby, are you okay? Can you move?" His expression is rapidly morphing into panic, which makes her laugh. It erupts from her like a bolt of lightning and soon enough, Oscar is laughing too. They both lay on the ground of the ice-skating rink, laughing hysterically. After a few moments, a clerk skates over and asks them if they are all right, which to his bewilderment, makes them laugh even harder.

For the first time in a long time, Abby feels a little less wound up inside, as though a tiny amount of pressure has been released. After ice skating, she and Oscar walk around outside and talk about life and their dreams. They hold hands with sparkling eyes and rosy cheeks from the early winter chill.

Chapter 41

They stand over the bed looking down at him, the intruder. There is no room for him in Abby's life and he's not trustworthy, but Abby is blinded by the way he makes her feel. Warm. Safe. No!

It's their job to keep Abby safe. That means protecting her from outsiders, and they are good at their job.

Chapter 42

Abby wakes up rested, happy. She rolls over to see Oscar, still asleep and snoring lightly, beside her. She studies his fully relaxed face, mouth hanging open and all, and she smiles. It's a good face.

She gets up and heads to the kitchen to make coffee, but something stops her on the way. There is a light emanating from her office and the door is slightly ajar. She opens the door tentatively. Her eyes immediately flicker over to the closet door. It's closed. She notices that all the curtains are pushed open though, which is odd. She usually keeps them closed tight.

The room is bathed in early morning light and the desk lamp is on. The light from the lamp is shining down on something on the desk. It's a photo of her as a child. It was taken right before it happened. Abby picks up the photo. The tape has been peeled away from the edges, but the marks are still there, silent reminders of where it used to hang – the back wall in her closet.

This is no coincidence. Someone is trying to tell her that they know what happened to her and about her secret obsession. They have also been in her house, while she's asleep. The realization makes Abby's

LITTLE FOXES

blood run cold. There is only one person she can think of who would've had easy access to her closet and he's currently sleeping peacefully in her bed.

Abby sneaks silently into the bedroom, scanning the area for his things. His backpack and clothes are lying on the floor next to the bed where he is still soundly asleep. She crawls on all fours over to his side of the bed, trying not to make any noise. Once there, she crouches on the floor, like a rabid animal, searching through his jean pockets and every crevice of the backpack.

She finds mostly normal items. Wallet, car keys, a few weathered cookbooks with mystery sauces splattered all over the pages. The thought of Oscar pouring over the pages to learn a new recipe makes her smile and she almost loses her focus. But then, she finds something. It's something hard rolled up in a soft, velvety fabric.

She pulls it out and unrolls the fabric. Laying on the floor in front of her is a set of expertly sharpened knives. Abby's logical side reassures her that he is a chef, and this is normal, but the skeptical side can't help staring at a dark stain in the corner of the fabric that looks suspiciously like blood.

She doesn't know what to do. She needs to think, so she decides to go to the gym.

LITTLE FOXES

Once there, the music and the adrenaline of working out and stretching every muscle to its limit do help to soothe her anxiety a little. A menacing thought remains, though, as small as a whisper, lurking in the dark recesses of her mind.

By the time Abby is ready to go home, she realizes she's been working out for hours. When she opens the door to her apartment, she can tell immediately that he's not there. There is a stillness, a void, which comes with being left alone.

A note with her name scribbled on it sits on the kitchen counter. She snatches it up, and as she reads, her heart churns with indecision.

It says, Love – I'm assuming you went to the gym to work out. I have to go to the restaurant, but I didn't want you to return and wonder where I'd gone. See you later? –Oscar.

Chapter 43

She rifles through her mom's dresser drawers, looking for cash or valuables – anything that will get her drugs. Cocaine is the best, but she's not picky when she's this desperate. She just needs something to quiet the noise in her head.

When she comes across a photo at the bottom of one of the drawers, her heart skips a beat. It's the photo she thought her mother threw away. The only photo she ever had of her with her dad.

Anger wells up inside of her. So, her mother has kept this photo, the only link she has to her father, all to herself, all these years. There is also a twenty shoved into the drawer. She pockets both the cash and the photo.

Chapter 44

Abby sits on Oscar's couch. She is acutely aware of the warmth of his chest against her side and the way his arm is wrapped around her and his fingers gently brushing her arm. A week ago, she would've let his warm sensuality fill the dark places inside her, but now…she's just not sure if she trusts him. She knows how to fake being the perfect girlfriend, though. She has had years of practice. Casually dating, until she loses interest, and they eventually leave her, as they always do. Guys are both easily distracted and maintained. She just needs to keep up on her appearance, wear sexy underwear and constantly smile and hang on his every word. Piece of cake.

"I'm going to go to the powder room. I'll be right back", she says cheerfully while extricating herself from his strong arms. She kisses him on the forehead, letting her freshly washed strawberry scented hair fall over his face. She can feel his gaze following her, so she walks away with a slow, seductive sway to her hips. The cool metal of Oscar's phone, squeezed into the pocket of her tight jeans burns against her thigh.

When she gets to the bathroom, she locks the door and pulls the phone from her pocket. It is slick with her own sweat, and she loses

LITTLE FOXES

her grip on it. It fumbles awkwardly from her hands and just misses the toilet, bouncing off the seat and clattering to the floor. She curses under her breath and then freezes. Every cell in her body is alert and listening for movement outside the bathroom door. When it doesn't come, she relaxes, slides to the floor and picks up the phone eagerly.

She gets to work. She's done this before. He has one of those swipe patterns on his lock screen. She has watched him do it before when his fingerprint scanner is acting up. She connects the outside layer of dots in a square shape- presumably an O, for Oscar. With that accomplished, she first looks through his apps for social media. She hasn't been able to find him anywhere by his name, but he could be using an account under a different name.

She doesn't find anything, though. At least nothing that's been used in the past year. She moves on to his internet search history. There is a bunch of stuff about cooking and recipes- nothing interesting. Abby can feel the beads of sweat gathering on her forehead. She has to hurry before he becomes suspicious of how long she is taking. She goes through his folders. There is one labeled 'Mom'.

When she opens it, she feels the familiar tingling of success and shame creeping through her veins. There are instructions on visiting his mom at the Algrove Correctional Wellness Facility. Abby takes photos on her own phone of the important stuff and closes the folder. Running out of time, the last thing she opens are his messages. Her heart stops in her chest when she spots a familiar number.

She clicks on the conversation. She has to scroll up quite a bit to get to the beginning. She begins furiously snapping photos of the conversation from beginning to end. When a drop of moisture falls on her hand, she realizes that tears are streaming down her face.

She is startled by a soft knocking on the door. "Abby, are you okay? You've been in there a while."

She lets out the long breath she's been holding. "I'll be out in a minute," she says, trying to keep her voice calm. She wipes the tears from her cheeks, then flushes the toilet. She splashes cold water over her face at the sink. She leans on the sides, steadying her shaking hands. "Pull yourself together," she whispers to her splotchy reflection, but she knows she won't be able to salvage this night after what she's seen.

Abby opens the door. Oscar is standing a few feet away. She can tell he has been pacing because he always runs his fingers through his hair when he does and right now, it is sticking up in every direction. "I'm so sorry," she says, trying hard to meet his eyes. "I think I might be coming down with something. It's probably best if I just go home."

LITTLE FOXES

Concern crosses over Oscar's features. "Is everything okay. Is there anything I can do?"

"No," she protests, and then dials it back a little. "There was a woman at the supermarket the other day who sneezed on me. I'm sure it's just a cold, but I don't want to get you sick, too. She forces herself to look him in the eyes. Willing him to believe her with her own.

"Okay," he concedes. "I'll let you go, get some rest, but don't worry about me, I'm as strong as an ox." He grabs her arm and pulls her into a hug, enveloping her. She lays her ear against his chest, listening to the rhythm of his steady heartbeat. For a moment, she feels so safe and comfortable that she contemplates staying and forgetting everything. His mom, the letters, but then the words from the cell phone screen come crashing back into her mind. She takes his phone from her own pocket and slips it into his, just as he lets her go.

She kisses him lightly on the cheek. "I'll see you later."

As Abby walks to her car, she puts her hand in her pocket, feeling her phone in anticipation. Later, when she's tucked in bed, she will look at every word, dissecting and deconstructing every possible meaning. Her brain pulses, buzzing in her skull. All she can think on the way back to her apartment is, why is Oscar texting my mom?

Chapter 45

Wes Conrad resembles his cousin in some ways, but not in others. He is bald, but he sports a jaunty mustache and is generally much smaller than Lee. Overall, he's been very amiable, a little jittery- in an ex-addict kind of way, but willing to talk to Davis and help out in any way he can.

"Lee told me that you two used to be pretty close, when you were little", says Davis, sipping from the mug of hot tea in front of him. Steam emits from the mug, which warms his hand when he lifts it to his mouth. It is comforting.

Wes nods and laughs a little. "Yeah, there was a time that I worshipped him, followed him around a lot like a beat animal that just doesn't learn."

"He also mentioned William Beaumont."

Davis notices a slight nervous tick in Wes's left cheek. His face flushes, possibly due to embarrassment, but Davis also can't help but notice how his demeanor changes. His features and muscles seem to sag, and a weariness takes over his body. "Bill", he says softly. "He died six years ago…cancer."

LITTLE FOXES

Davis shifts in his seat. He has stumbled across perhaps the biggest difference between Lee and Wes. Lee comes across as if he's constantly trying to control the narrative and stay one step ahead of him at all times. The man before him, however, is made up of raw emotion. He is wearing his heart fully on his sleeve. "I'm sorry for your loss," says Davis, and then adds, "I can see that you were close. Would you like to tell me about him?"

Wes pulls his glasses from his face and wipes the wet tears from his eyes with the back of his hand. "Bill was the only person who truly cared about me," he says through sniffles. "I was a lonely kid. My father hated me. My mother ignored me. Everyone treated me like a nuisance, like I wasn't welcome. I always got the feeling they were ashamed of me."

His face reddens again, but he continues. "There was this pond near our house. I used to go there and skip stones, fish, stuff like that. One day, when I was there, just hangin out by myself, this little yappy dog came up out of nowhere and started barking at me. It had real curly hair, all in its face. I thought it looked funny, so I started laughing at it. Then, I heard him calling out, Henry, henry, where are you, before I saw him. When he ran up, all sweaty and out of breath, I could immediately tell he was different. Like not from around there."

"How could you tell," asks Davis.

LITTLE FOXES

"Well mainly because he was dressed nicely. He was wearing button-down shirt and nice slacks. Not the type of thing people generally wore in those parts. I told him I had never seen such a small, yappy dog before and he thought that was interesting.

He smiled at me, but not in a way like he was looking down on me, but like he was genuinely interested in what I had to say. We talked the whole day. He told me about all the places he had visited. I told him I'd never been nowhere. Then he said he was leaving in two days and asked if I wanted to come.

I did think it was a little strange, since he was older, fifty-two, and... the way he looked at me, I did kind of wonder if he wanted something more from me. He was so nice to me though, so, I don't know...I told him I would think about it. Then, when I thought about it, it occurred to me that no one would even care if I left...so I did."

Wes pauses to sip his own tea thoughtfully.

After a moment, he adjusts his glasses, which had slid down onto the bridge of his nose and continues. "I know what you're probably thinking," says Wes, meeting Davis's gaze directly. "But Bill was good to me. He treated me much better than my own kin ever did. He took me places, gave me culture...and I loved him for it."

LITTLE FOXES

Davis nods. An understanding passes between the two men. Davis clears his throat. "Your cousin, Lee, said that when you came back, you were fifteen and quite the ladies' man. He said you bragged about luring some young girls from the mall."

Wes just blankly stares at him, seemingly unsure of how to respond. The crimson flush returns to his cheeks.

"Do you remember hearing about the disappearance of two young girls- the fox sisters- around that time? The last place they were seen alive was the Turner Hill Mall."

Chapter 46

Abby wakes up groggily. She must have fallen asleep on the couch again. She wipes the drool and tears from her face as a noise echoes and eventually registers in her brain. It's the landline. She walks on rubbery legs to the phone, hanging on the wall, in the kitchen. She picks it up off the receiver but doesn't lift it to her ear. Instead, she bangs the phone four times against the kitchen counter. Each time harder than the last. Then she hangs it up and waits. A moment later, it starts to ring again. She picks it up on the third ring and lifts it to her ear, wordlessly.

"Abby!" Her mom's voice sounds high-pitched and erratic. Then, when there is no response, it morphs into a question, "Abby? Abby, are you there?"

She can feel the anger burning in her cheeks. She screams into the phone. "Why are you texting Oscar behind my back?" Then she hangs it up violently and grabs the phone cradle, pulling with both hands until it separates from the wall, snapping the cord. She throws it down on the floor with a loud crash and then falls to the floor herself, pressing her hot cheek against the cold linoleum.

LITTLE FOXES

About five minutes later, her cell phone vibrates loudly on the floor next to her. She looks at the screen. It's a text. From her mom:

I texted Oscar because I was worried about you. You haven't answered your phone or returned any of my calls for a week now. I need to know that you are okay.

Abby lays there on the hard kitchen floor until the arm that is tucked beneath her starts to go numb. Then, she forces herself to stand and makes her way to the bedroom, like a zombie, just going through the motions. She lays flat on the floor beside the bed and reaches her arm underneath, pulling out a well-worn shoebox.

She removes the lid, which is frayed and torn at the edges. Inside is a collection of items- rubber bands, safety pins, and rusty razor blades. She caresses the items, running her fingers carefully across them and welcoming them like old friends. When they catch on to a folded-up newspaper with worn edges, she grabs at it and pulls it from the box. She unfolds it with extreme care. The heavy creases tell a story of this exact motion being repeated multiple times.

Abby's breath catches in her throat, however when the paper is completely unfolded, lying flat on her lap. She holds it up in front of her. The date at the top of the page is from twenty years ago. She bought it online. It is the newspaper from when they went missing. But now, in the center of the page is a gaping hole, where the article has been cut out. She knows the missing words by heart, but the loss still cuts her deeply.

Abby throws the paper down and runs back to the kitchen. She kneels in front of the trash can, praying that it's not already gone. She can't remember taking the garbage out this week. She pulls out everything from wet coffee grounds to balled up tissues until it's all heaped in a smelly pile in the middle of the kitchen floor, but it's not there. She leans back against the kitchen cabinets and closes her eyes, deflated.

When she opens them again, however, they land on something under the table by the window. It's a small piece of paper, caught under the table leg, fluttering gently back and forth from the air streaming out of the heat vent on the floor.

Abby crawls over energetically and snatches it up, then stumbles back to the bedroom. She presses the clipping into the hole on the newspaper and then sits back. It's a perfect fit. Only one person that Abby knows of has been in her apartment, her bedroom…Oscar.

Chapter 47

Wes Conrad's expression is one of pure surprise. Then, as realization sets in, Davis watches as his features slowly transform into an expression of deep sadness. "He said that? His voice is trembling and childlike. He twists his body in the seat, away from Davis, and quickly wipes away the tears that are glistening on his cheeks.

Davis sips his tea, giving him a moment to compose himself. Then, as if a thought has occurred to him, Wes straightens in his chair and asks, "When did this happen?"

The girls were last seen on Easter weekend, April 2004, answers Davis. A lightbulb seems to go off in Wes's mind, brightening his features. He stands and leaves the room without another word. He returns, however, a moment later with a photo album in his hands. He sits at the table and opens it, turning the pages feverishly. When he finds the one he's looking for he stops and yells, "Aha, I knew it", pointing his finger at a photo on the page.

He passes the album to Davis who looks at the photo. It is of a teenage boy laying in a bed, wrapped up in a full body cast. His face is bruised black and blue, but there is a look in his eyes that reminds

Davis of the man sitting before him. Underneath the photo is an inscription- Wes after barn accident, March 31st, 2004.

"When I came home that year, I visited my parents, but my dad was a total asshole and we got into an argument. I climbed up to the barn roof, like I used to do a lot when I was angry. It was a big two-story barn that was old and rotting, just like everything else on that property. I fell through the roof and ended up breaking nine different bones. I was holed up in a full body cast like that for four whole months. I couldn't go anywhere, let alone the mall.

Chapter 48

Davis sits at his desk, contemplating his conversation with Wes Conrad. His alibi for the time of the girls' disappearance was corroborated by medical records from his time in the hospital. Why did Lee try to pin the kidnapping and probable murder of two young girls on his own cousin, who, by his own account, looked up to him?

Davis's skin starts to crawl as he thinks about all the time he's spent interviewing Lee and listening to his lies. To Lee, this seems to be no more than a game. Davis puts his elbows on the desk and runs his hands through his thinning hair. He's not sure how much longer he can take this.

As he lifts his elbows off the desk, some of the papers that were scattered beneath them go fluttering to the floor. Davis leans over to pick them up, but as he does, one of them catches his eye. It looks too thick, like there might be something behind it. Sure enough, as Davis picks up the paper and examines it, he can see that there is another page stuck to it. He separates the pages carefully.

As he looks at the new page, his heartbeat speeds up rapidly. He is staring at a sketch artist photo of a man in his late teens to early

LITTLE FOXES

twenties with greasy shoulder-length hair and side-swept bangs. It is labelled 'staring man at mall'. The writing is faded. The page is sticky and stained with what looks like splotches of mustard. The face staring up at Davis is much younger than the one he is used to looking at, but it is, nevertheless, unmistakable. It is the face of Lee Conrad.

Davis gapes at the drawing before him with a million thoughts racing through his brain. He is startled by the phone when it rings.

"Detective Davis," he answers, robotically.

"Hi, I am agent Tom Mills with the FBI. I believe you've been interviewing Lee Conrad in connection to a missing persons case?"

"Yes," says Davis, stunned.

"Well, if he's not already your main suspect, I believe you may want to take a harder look at him. We have reason to believe that he was involved in the disappearance of some young girls in Fort Worth, Texas while he lived there in 2005."

Chapter 49

Someone is ringing the doorbell. The thought shoots into Abby's brain like a torpedo. "What now," she thinks, shaking off her dazed state to stand and answer the door. She rubs her hands on her pant legs. They feel sticky for some reason.

She looks out the peep hole first. There is no one there. She opens the door to see a package on her doorstep. She grabs a pair of scissors from the kitchen and cuts open the massive amount of tape holding the box together. Confusion tinged with fear swells within her as she removes the contents and places it on the kitchen counter before her.

It is a stuffed animal. A possum to be precise. Abby's mind flashes back to her childhood, but she pushes the thought away. There is a pocket, or pouch, on the possum's belly.

Abby slowly reaches her hand into the pocket. She isn't sure what exactly she was expecting to find there. A baby possum, perhaps? What she does pull out though, shocks her to her core. It is the photograph of her as a baby with her real father. She was sure she had hidden it away, but here it is, stuffed inside a possum's stomach.

LITTLE FOXES

She turns the photo over. Magazine letters are glued to the back, spelling out the words those two dreaded words. I KNOW.

She feels sick. The acid in her stomach churns. Her head swims with confusion and fear. This is more depraved than she ever expected. This person knows things about her and is twisting them up like gnarled and knotted tree limbs for their own amusement. A darkness begins to creep into the edges of her vision. This ends now, she thinks.

Chapter 50

Only a small trace of the woman from the photo in Oscar's apartment remains in the elderly woman sitting across from Abby. Her eyes, a shadow of what they once were, stare vacantly ahead of her, without really looking at anything. Abby introduced herself as Oscar's 'serious girlfriend' twenty minutes ago, without so much as a flicker of recognition from her, and the two of them have been sitting in mind-numbing silence ever since.

According to Abby's research, this woman, Violet, had been vibrant once, and quite beautiful. She went down a path of drugs and prostitution, though, which landed her in jail on multiple occasions. Abby wonders what happened to Oscar during those times.

Five years ago, she was once again arrested for drug possession and was incarcerated here- Algrove Correctional Wellness facility- due to her dementia diagnosis. It reminds Abby of some of the mental health facilities she has checked into in the past. You have a roommate, but your own private bathroom and there are no cages, just doors that lock from the outside.

LITTLE FOXES

Now, sitting across from this feeble shell of a woman, Abby wonders if she made a mistake visiting her. What if she is just jumping to conclusions about Oscar having anything to do with the newspaper clipping, the letters and the photo? Even if he did, is there any information to be had from this woman?

"Oscar is doing well," says Abby, trying her luck. He really enjoys being a chef…and he talks about you all the time," She adds the last part hoping to spark some emotion in the woman and for a moment, she thinks she just might have. Violet's eyes seem to flutter towards her and rest on her own eyes, for just half a second. Abby considers it progress. "Oh yeah, he is constantly saying how much he misses you."

"Stop that man," Violet yells, suddenly, pointing her finger towards the door. "He stole my teeth!" Abby turns around just in time to see a male employee rush past the open door, as if his life depends on avoiding confrontation with this woman. Abby sighs and begins collecting her bag from the floor. This was a bad idea.

When she looks back up at Violet to say her goodbyes, she finds the old woman looking intently back at her. For the moment, the clouds seem to have parted and her sparkling amber eyes are shining through. She holds out her bony arm, beckoning Abby to come closer. Abby kneels next to her chair and the old woman places her hand on top of hers. Her skin is wrinkled and cold, but her grip is surprisingly firm. A shiver of anticipation runs down Abby's spine. "Don't trust him," she practically spits out. Then, just as suddenly, she loosens her hold on Abby and relaxes in her chair, returning her gaze to some far-off place.

Those three words cement Abby's suspicions.

Chapter 51

Davis stands next to Agent Tom Mills who is slender and tall, well over six feet. Davis has to incline his head upwards to make eye contact with him. The two of them are looking through a two-way mirror into an adjoining room. Inside the room, Lee sits, handcuffed to a table and looking a little sour at being kept waiting. That was Tom's idea.

"I want to get a good look at him before you go in," he had said. "I like to observe how they react to stress." Lee is reacting angrily. Every so often, he looks over at the mirror with a bitter scowl.

"You sure you don't want to take the lead on this," asks Davis.

"Positive," he answers, still looking at Lee. Then he turns towards Davis and smiles reassuringly down at him. "You have built up a rapport with him. He trusts you, and from what I can tell, that doesn't happen very often. You'll do fine. Try to stick to the talking points but do what comes naturally." He places a hand on Davis's shoulder. "We're gonna get him."

LITTLE FOXES

Davis inhales a long breath of air and then exhales. He squares his shoulders and then walks through the door into the room where Lee is waiting.

Davis sets the photo down on the table in front of Lee. "Do you remember when your cousin, Wes, fell through the barn roof?" A flicker of something, recognition or maybe uneasiness, flashes momentarily across Lee's features.

"He had to go to the hospital and was in a full body cast for four months," Davis continues. "Now, do you remember when that was?" Lee continues to stare straight ahead, without any reaction or hint of an intention to speak.

"It was in the spring of 2004, the same time as the disappearance of the Fox sisters."

Lee looks down, studying the photo. Davis can almost see the wheels turning in his brain. Then, Lee looks up at him and breaks into a broad mischievous grin. It throws Davis off a little. He tries to re-balance his emotions as Lee finally begins to talk.

"Have you ever seen a fox in the wild?" Davis shakes his head in response. "You'll hear them first. When they are scared, or cornered, they will scream. It almost sounds like a person screaming." Lee lets that thought settle for a moment, then continues.

"When I was little, before all the foster homes, my father used to get blind drunk just about every night. He would beat the shit out of me for a while, but at some point, he would get tired and pass out. That's when I would sneak out of the house and go exploring in the woods.

Nature comes alive at night, in a way that it don't during the day. I liked knowing that – feeling like I was experiencing something that few people ever did. Foxes are 'specially hard to get close to. They are small and fast, and they warn each other when there's danger. It's best to find their den during the day and then go back to it at night. Then you just sit very still and wait. Eventually they will come out to play."

Davis is stunned and truly disturbed. Who is this person sitting two feet across the table from him? "Lee, if you can see the beauty in nature like that, you obviously have emotions. There's a mother and a father out there, hearts shattered into a million pieces, a shell of who they once were, because after twenty long years, they still don't know what happened to their only daughters." Davis knows this is, once again, a long shot, but he doesn't know what else to do. He has to reach this husk of a person sitting before him somehow and make him feel something. Shame, worry…hell, even anger would be better than this.

LITTLE FOXES

Lee looks down at his hands. "I know I should be worried about the girls, the family putting it to rest and all that, but you also gotta look at it like…" He pauses, seemingly struggling to find the right words. "I'm a survivor…what's gonna happen to me? My good for nothing father is dead, but there is one person who is still alive who could hurt me. Even in here. I'm more afraid of him than I am of going to hell."

Davis looks at his file. Tom had given him extensive notes on the various eclectic members of Lee's family tree. Most of the males, and some of the females, have been in prison at least once in their lives. Lee's father, Gregory Conrad and his brother, Lee's uncle, Benjamin Conrad, are the two most notorious of the bunch. Burglary, battery and assault with a deadly weapon being just of few of the crimes that have sent them yo-yoing in and out of prison for most of their lives. "Are you referring to your uncle, Benjamin," asks Davis.

"He's not a good man," says Lee.

"Look Lee, I'm going to level with you because I think you can handle it", says Davis. "Right now, all roads are leading to you, and that's where it dead- ends. If you have any information or saw anything, you need to tell me now, so that we can put the right man behind bars."

LITTLE FOXES

Lee sighs and closes his eyes tight as he speaks. "Daddy and uncle Benji always talked about getting into that business, girls…porn. They said they knew a guy – a guy with a bum leg- who was gonna teach them all about how to get away with it.

I didn't think they'd actually do it, but then one day, my father called me up and said he needed me and Nancy to babysit for him."

"That's Nancy Pritchard? Your girlfriend at the time?"

"Yes. I thought he was talkin crazy, but when we went over there, sure enough, there were two little girls, in the basement. They were dirty and the little one kept cryin and rubbin snot everywhere. We watched em for about an hour. Nancy tried to talk to em, but the older one was real sleepy and, like I said, the little one was cryin, the whole time."

"Can you describe the room that you saw the girls in?"

"It was a basement, but it was separated into two rooms. The room they were in had old green carpeting on the floor and a matching green couch."

"Can you describe the other room?"

"The other room was smaller and had a bare floor. It was like a cellar room. It didn't have light. As far as I know it was always used to store boxes and stuff. I think at one time, it was all one big space, but someone or other had put up a shitty wall to make another room there.

"Did you ask your father why he had the girls there, or why they were so upset?"

Lee nods. "He said to mind my own business, but that they had gone with him willingly when he offered them weed, and then, soon as they got what they wanted, they turned sour, like the little cunts that they were."

Davis is momentarily shocked but regains his composure. It's not uncommon for male criminals to describe women, even girls, that way. Davis pulls the sketch artist photo from his file folder and sets it down on the table in front of Lee. "Do you know what this is?"

Lee just shrugs his shoulders.

"It is a sketch of a man who was seen staring at the girls on the day they disappeared at the mall. That's you, right?"

Lee looks crestfallen. "All right," he says. "I was there that day. I just didn't want to tell you because I felt ashamed."

"Why?"

LITTLE FOXES

"I didn't want anyone gettin the wrong idea. Yeah, I was lookin at them and following them, but that was because my father and uncle were there too, and I was worried."

"Why were you worried?"

"I don't know, it was just a feeling," Lee says, red-faced. "With how much they'd been talkin about young girls lately, but I had to go to work, so I left, but my father and uncle stayed. That's why I went in to the police station. I wanted to tell someone, but…I just lost my nerve."

Chapter 52

Detective Davis and Agent Tom Mills walk through the small old house that Lee grew up in. Gregory Welch's widow begrudgingly let them in to look around. There's not much to it. The living room, kitchen and dining room are all one space. There is one small bathroom and one normal- sized bedroom. There is another very small room, presumably Lee's bedroom growing up. Everything is on the same level. There doesn't appear to be an entrance to a basement anywhere. Tom shoots Davis a wary glance.

"Where is your basement," Davis asks the woman in his pleasantest voice.

"Ain't no basement. Shed's out back."

"Sorry…there is no basement at all?"

"Did I stutter," she shoots back, her face drawn into a strickening scowl.

Behind the house, Davis and Tom inspect the wooden shed. It's actually more of a lean-to. One side is made up of scrap metal. The doorway has no actual door on it and the floor is made up of earth and dirt. It is nothing like the basement that Lee described.

"Should we check his uncle's house? Maybe he was mistaken."

"What about the address where Lee was living with his girlfriend at the time", replies Tom.

Davis opens his file folder. "I've got it here. Big Creek road, maybe a twenty minute drive from here."

"Let's check it out."

Roughly half an hour later, they are staring at a room that looks exactly like the one that Lee described. The couch has been removed, but it looks like the frayed green carpet remains on the bigger space. The wooden make-shift wall is still there as well, creating another small room that could only be described as a dungeon. It is dark and rank.

"Over here. Look at this," says Tom from the big room. He is pointing to a stain on the once green carpet, making it look black in that one spot. "Could be blood."

Davis's stomach turns. Deep in his gut he knows that this is where the girls were held and maybe even where they died. He suddenly feels like crying. He struggles to keep his voice even, but he fails and

LITTLE FOXES

it cracks emotionally. "He lied to me. He just…keeps on lying to me. I don't know, I just don't think I can get him to confess."

Tom smiles and places a comforting hand on Davis's back. "It's okay. We don't need him to confess. He fucked up and described the room where he kept them in great detail and it was the basement of his own residence. It's just a matter of connecting the dots, but…I think we got him."

Davis exhales the breath that he didn't realize he was holding in. Relief floods every vein. It's warm and heavy, like a heated blanket.

"We got him."

Chapter 53

She rides her bike and it feels like flying. She lifts her arms at her sides and just coasts. The warm summer breeze tickles the bare skin. She closes her eyes and trusts gravity and the wheels and the road to move her forward. This is heaven.

A car horn blares loudly behind her, jolting her back into reality. She veers to the side of the road to let the car pass. The old woman shakes her head violently, judging her from inside the car.

She is about to return to the road when she spots a big white van across the street. There is a guy, maybe late teens - older than her, leaning against the side of the van, smoking a cigarette. He is looking at her. Then, he throws the cigarette on the ground and smiles, waving at her. She waves back.

Chapter 54

Laura wakes groggily. She can't seem to focus her eyes and her head aches with a throbbing pain. She tries to stand, but her right ankle buckles underneath her. When she touches the skin there, it is sensitive and swollen. She moves her hands to the floor. It seems to be made of dirt and there is a musty smell in the air. It's like the smell of the little cellar room where her mother keeps her jars of canned vegetables. A shiver runs through her body. It's so cold.

She tries to look around, but the room is dark. She still sleeps with a nightlight at home. She remembers her sister's taunting words when her parents put it in for her, "What a baby. How can you sleep with all that light?" Michelle never needed a night light.

Where is Michelle? Panic rises in her chest. She tries to scream, but her voice is hoarse, and she ends up coughing instead. She struggles to produce enough spit to loosen up her aching vocal cords. Finally, after a little while, she can call out feebly. "Shell! Are you here, Shell?" She repeats her cry, getting a little louder each time. Until…she hears something.

LITTLE FOXES

Through the darkness, she can hear a noise. She turns her body and slides slowly on her hands and knees until she runs into something, banging the top of her head. She puts her hands out in front of her. It's a wall.

"Shell," she yells desperately. A sob hitches in her throat as she listens for a response. Then she hears it. Three quick knocks, followed by two slow ones. It's their secret knock. Laura knocks back, desperate. Moments later, she can hear Michelle's faint voice.

"Lor, are you okay?" Her voice is excruciatingly weak, barely above a whisper.

"I think so," says Laura, "Are you?"

There is a slight pause. "I'm fine…Do you remember anything?"

Laura rubs her temples, trying to remember. "The mall…we went to the mall, but where are we now? How did we get here?"

"We are in some kind of basement, but in different rooms…are you sure you don't remember anything else?"

"Nnn…No…should I?"

"No, that's good. You're okay, it's going to be okay. What does dad always say?"

LITTLE FOXES

"Foxes don't give up", says Laura smiling. She can almost feel the sudden relief radiating from Michelle through the wall. She puts her hand against the wall, imagining that she can feel Michelle's hand in her own. Her teeth begin to chatter. She pulls her knees up to her chin, hugging them, and leans her head against the wall. Somewhere in the abyss, there is a leaky pipe. Drip… Drip… Drip. The sound echoes in her brain as she falls into exhausted sleep.

Chapter 55

The doorbell won't stop ringing. And then, someone is standing over her. The thick fog of memory clears enough for Abby to recognize her mother and the fact that she does not look happy.

Abby groans. "How did you get in?"

"That's all you have to say to me," huffs her mother. I have been calling you nonstop. At first it just gave an endless busy signal, and then…it switched to one of those high-pitched out of service tones. So I tried your cell, which just goes straight to a voicemail that is full. And then, having had enough, I decided to come over, you know just to check that you're still alive, but you weren't answering the door either, so I used my key and here you are, taking a nap."

"I'm sorry… you used your key?"

Her mother puts her hands on her hips and looks down at Abby defensively. "I had a key made, for emergencies, and it's a good thing I did too." She sits on the bed and seems to soften a little. "Is everything all right?"

LITTLE FOXES

Abby tries to grasp those words. All right. Nothing is all right. What even is right anyways? She can't say any of that to her mom, though. She just wouldn't understand. Or would she? Tears begin to well in her eyes as she contemplates what it would be like to just tell her mother everything right now. Would she be supportive and take some of Abby's burden from her, scooping it up in her arms and throwing it out the window? Or would her face transform into one of hatred and disgust?

Her mother looks down at her own hands and doesn't notice the tears in her daughter's eyes. "Oscar is worried about you too."

The words send off explosions throughout Abby's brain, and then, they leak out. She flings herself off the bed and practically jumps to the other side of the room, far from her mom. "Do not say that name to me," she says through gritted teeth.

Her mother looks shocked. "Honey, I just don't understand what he did that's so bad. Please tell me."

"He's stalking me and sending me threatening letters," Abby screams. Then she storms from the room and grabs the crumpled newspaper article, only to return and fling it at her mother.

Her mother looks at the article and then her face seems to age instantly. She looks deflated and sad. Why is she sad? Why is she not mad? "Sweetheart, I think you need to go back to therapy. Are you taking your medication?"

Abby is stricken by the words. She can't understand the question or why her mom is asking it. She runs to the bathroom and closes herself inside, slamming the door and locking it behind her. She sits with her back against the door and cries as her mother bangs on it, yelling or quietly speaking muffled words intermittently. Abby can't hear or understand any of it. Then, finally, after what feels like forever, the noise stops, and the apartment seems to grow cold. Abby is alone.

Chapter 56

Mark Davis sits in his garage, nursing a beer. It's the only place where he feels alone enough to think. He knows that Lee is lying, but to what extent? He needs to find a way to connect all the dots.

A few minutes later, the garage goes dark. His wife must have flipped the light switch from inside the house. She knows he sits out here, but that's her way of saying she's going to bed now and she doesn't care. It's almost funny how they've learned to communicate recently without actually communicating.

Davis doesn't move, however. He is deep in thought and whether dark or light, he can't break his concentration. He will sit in this spot and think until he either has a breakthrough, or passes out on the floor from exhaustion.

Chapter 57

"So, you lured them from the mall and then kept them at your place for your father and uncle…why?"

Lee shifts and Detective Davis can see that 'wheels turning' expression that he has come to know the past few months. "I already told you, they wanted to get into that game. They told me to get them girls…young girls. They aint the type you say no to."

"What game did they want to get into?"

"Sex…porn…I told you all this before."

"I know, Lee, but we don't have any evidence that your father and uncle were involved in this. So it's on me to make sure that what you're telling me is gonna hold up in front of a judge. Cause, we're in this thing now, you and me. This train is moving and there's no getting off. Do you understand me?"

Lee rubs a patch of dry skin on his bald head. "What if I told you that I saw my uncle 'with' the older one?"

"I would ask you to tell me more…and be specific."

LITTLE FOXES

"Well, I went down there one day…after I picked up them girls."

"To the basement?"

"Yeah, my father was standing there with one of them camcorder-things. He was filming my uncle having sex with the older one. She was awake, but not all there- like she was drugged."

Chapter 58

"He's still lying to me!" Davis throws the file folder he's holding across the room. Papers fly out and land everywhere, fluttering to the floor.

"It's okay," says Tom, placing a hand on his shoulder, sending a tiny jolt of electricity through his arm. "I've got something. Turns out Lee has another cousin who owns property in Virginia. Land in the mountains. It seems a few months after the kidnappings some of the neighbors started complaining about a bonfire on the property. Apparently, it was burning all day and night, and several people described a stench like rotting flesh."

Chapter 59

"First and last name?"

"Lacie Dalton".

"It says here your first name is Abby."

"Yes…I changed it…from Lacie."

"Okay, why don't you tell me what happened between you and the defendant…Lee Conrad." Assistant district Attorney, Vivian Perez, looks at her expectantly. Her features are drenched in pity, which unnerves Abby.

She shifts in her seat, feeling the heat rise in her face. "Could I have a glass of water," she asks, hoarsely.

Some of the pity in the woman's face seems to shift into something more like annoyance, but she keeps her voice even. "Of course." She presses a button on the phone receiver. "Melinda, could you please bring a glass of water for Ms. Dalton."

Moments later, Abby takes the water down in a few feverish gulps. Then, she begins.

LITTLE FOXES

"Lee Conrad abducted me when I was twelve."

Vivian Perez is hooked. The curiosity inside her becomes a palpable thing sitting between them. Abby likes that it's there. It obstructs her view of the woman's judgmental eyes. Vivian grabs a pen and a legal pad from her desk and begins scribbling notes, as Abby continues.

"It was in Clearville, PA…where I grew up. I was riding my bike on this road near our house. I can't remember what it was called, but I used to ride my bike there all the time". Abby closes her eyes, remembering. "At this one spot, there was a wall of honeysuckle vines. In the springtime, they smelled so sweet. I used to reach up and pluck off the little white flowers and then suck on them as I rode. One day, he was there. He was across the road, leaning against his van and smoking."

"And you're sure that it was this man that you saw," asks Vivien, holding up one of Lee's older arrest photos.

"Yes, it was him. He was younger then, though, more boyish. He looked like everyone else around there. Like he was used to hard work, but he also had a mysteriousness about him. Something intangible, but intriguing. That first time, he just waved at me, but I started seeing him there constantly, in that same spot.

After a while, he became like a dependable thing that I could count on…and we started talking. It started as polite small talk, but before I knew it, I was telling him things about school and my parents, stuff like that. I thought he was my friend."

A fresh wave of nervousness washes over Abby, making her flush again. She ignores it this time, though. She told herself she would do this and see it through to the end. For them.

The pent-up words begins to tumble out of her mouth, gaining momentum.

"One day it was raining. I didn't usually go out in the rain, but my parents were fighting a lot and I just needed to get out of the house. When I got to our spot, though, he wasn't there. I was blindsided and upset. It just felt like the final straw, piled on top of all the other straws. And it was too much.

I left my bike and took off running into the woods. I was looking for nothing, but also for him in a way, I guess. And then I saw the van. It was parked at the end of a little clearing. I remember that it suddenly felt wrong being there. Like- what was I doing? Out there in the middle of the woods, looking for someone I barely knew.

The inappropriateness just all dawned on me at once…but it was too late. He had seen me. It was one of those big work vans with two doors that open outward on the back. He had been sitting back there with the doors open. He called my name and started approaching me like I was a skittish animal. I kind of felt like one, too. Like I was

LITTLE FOXES

stuck in place, not knowing if I should stay or bolt. I was very aware, though, that I had no idea where I was or how to get home. So, I stayed.

He gave me some kind of alcohol, whiskey I think, and a blanket. I knew it was wrong, but I just didn't want to feel sad anymore. We sat in the back of his van, which is when I realized that he was living in it. I think he might've drugged me too. I started getting tired and I lost consciousness. When I came to, I was laying on my stomach. I could barely move. My ankles and wrists were tied."

Abby looks up at Vivien, briefly, then back down at her feet. "He raped me…but I got away."

Vivien's face has now become serious and perplexed. "When did you or your parents report the rape," she asks, flipping through some of the papers in front of her on her desk.

"They didn't- I didn't. When, I saw on the news that he was being charged with the abduction and murder of those two little girls, I knew I needed to say something to someone."

Vivien's face crumples a little and the look of pity returns. "Thank you for sharing that information with me Ms. Dalton. You've been very helpful. I will be in touch."

LITTLE FOXES

Abby is ushered out of the building and sent on her way. A few months later, she receives a typed letter from Vivien Perez explaining that while they are grateful for the information she shared, her testimony will not be required in court since the events that transpired over twenty years earlier, between her and Lee Conrad, could not be corroborated.

Chapter 60

"I can't believe that you're doing this to me, I just walked em out of the mall, got em in the car, so I'm guilty of that. Give me twenty years if that's what's going to happen, ya know. I'm guilty of that. That's as far as I'm guilty of."

Detective Davis wipes the sweat from his brow. This thing is going to trial. It will be out of his hands in a matter of weeks. They have meticulously built a strong case against Lee…but Davis still can't help but to want to hear the words come out of his wicked mouth…I did it.

"This is me doing my job," he says to Lee, "and this is you trying to figure out a way to explain what you saw, what your involvement was and what we can prove and disprove. And I hope that makes sense to you."

"Yeah, it does," replies Lee wearily. "You're a cop but you're a good guy. You have a good heart. But I can't say anything that's gonna implicate me even more."

Later that evening, Davis and Tom sit next to one another at a bar. Davis nurses his beer, feeling especially sulky.

LITTLE FOXES

"Come on man," says Tom in a soothing voice. The ADA has picked up the case. She wouldn't have done that if she didn't have faith in the evidence. The evidence that you put together. You should be proud of yourself." He raises his beer bottle towards Davis.

Davis reluctantly raises his own and clinks the glass against Tom's bottle. The next few hours are a blur of more drinks and congratulation until Davis's thinking starts to shift. He knows that he did his best. Maybe Tom is right, and he just needs to trust the state to do their part.

When he ends up in the bathroom with Tom at the end of the night, it is thrilling, but it also kind of feels like finally finding a shoe that fits and doesn't cause any pain. He wants to hold on to that feeling forever.

Chapter 61

Abby sits on the edge of her bed, mentally preparing herself for what is to come. The trial of Gregory Lee Conrad. It has been looming over her as a shadow in the corner of her eyeline for years. Nothing is more important than this. It is the culmination of all her fears and anguish over the years. She needs to put everything with Oscar and the threats out of her mind so that she can focus and keep it together long enough to see this through to the end.

Chapter 62

"Good morning, my name is Vivian Perez, and I am the prosecutor in this case. It is my pleasure to represent the people of this state. On April 10th, 2004- Easter weekend, four young girls went to the mall to look at the Easter decorations. Two of those girls never made it home because the defendant in this case took them to his house, kept them in the basement, performed unspeakable acts of violence on them- some sexual in nature- and then ended their short lives, taking the bodies to a family residence and burning them on a bonfire for days, emitting the unmistakable fumes of rotting flesh."

Chapter 63

Abby sits in the back of the court room. She stares at the back of his bald head. She hasn't been this close to him in years. Her head buzzes with excitement and she can barely take in what is happening.

She also spots another familiar face sitting in the galley in front of her. It is the lead cold case detective who helped bring all this to fruition. Abby has only seen photos of him online. She feels almost giddy sitting here in the same space as him. Only a short distance separating them.

Before she knows it, the opening statements are over and the trial is officially under way. She looks at the jury, wishing she were there among them. She looks at each of their faces, willing them with all her strength to see the man that sits before them for what he really is…a monster.

Chapter 64

Detective Davis sits in the courtroom, a few feet back from the prosecution table. Being a witness in the trial means that he will only be allowed to view certain parts of the proceedings. He listens to the opening statement of ADA Vivian Perez with great interest. All of his hard work, nearly two years ago now, has compounded to this thing. This trial. He has been retired for a year now. He is amicably divorced and spends his days cooking with his partner or renovating his 1972 Triumph Stag. His life is quiet. He is happy.

When he walked in the bustling court building this morning, it was a bit of a culture shock for him. Even so, he wouldn't miss this for the world. He looks over at Lee. He can see part of his profile from where he is sitting. Lee looks older, wearier, maybe even a little more pale. Davis looks to the jury box. He hopes that this pale old man sitting before them doesn't affect their perception of what he truly is deep down inside…a monster.

Chapter 65

She moves her book bag onto her back and braces herself to stand as soon as her stop comes into view. Even though it's still a way down the road, she wants to be ready to make her escape as quickly as possible. Her chubby, childlike fingers clutch the bus seat in front of her. She has trouble holding onto the slippery plastic material, so she digs her nails into it until the ends of her fingers turn pale.

She wouldn't have such a hard time if she wasn't always biting her nails. Her mother's chiding voice invades her thoughts.

It's time to focus. The spot where the school bus lets her out is now within view. It's a lonely tree-lined road. There is a patch of dirt on the roadside that is used as a bus stop for a cluster of children who live down the windy dirt roads of Clearville, Pennsylvania. Most of the parents park their vehicles in this little inlet and wait to pick up their children and spare them from having to walk the rest of the way. Lacie is not so lucky.

The brakes squeal as the bus lurches to a stop and Lacie is the first out of her seat. She glides to the front of the bus, laser focused on

LITTLE FOXES

the door. Then she hears the words that she dreads hearing every day.

"Eeeewwww! What's that smell!" The exclamation came from a girl in her class…Missy. She is a spoiled princess who does nothing but make Lacie's life a living hell. She hates her.

Right on cue, her words set off the other hecklers, who begin yelling things like, "Gross" and "take a shower," loudly in her direction.

Lacie trips on one of her shoelaces and stumbles slightly, which causes even more snickering to erupt from behind her. "Look at her dirty shoes," someone else yells, as if all her problems are somehow caused by the thick layer of dirt and mud on her shoes.

Holding back tears, she finally makes it off the bus and into the fresh air. She takes in a deep breath but is shoved forward by the other kids coming off the bus behind her.

She weaves between the cars until she is tucked away in the back corner of the inlet, where she waits. She has to cross the road to get to her house. Experience, though, has taught her that it's better to wait until all the cars have left, lest they don't see her and 'accidentally' run her off the road. In these moments her mind often imagines some nice parent seeing her there, smiling warmly, and then offering to drive her home. That never happens.

LITTLE FOXES

In a cluster of chaotic flashes, the cars zoom away in various directions, leaving a collective cloud of dust behind them. Lacie is left standing there, alone. She crosses the road and then begins the two-mile trek to her house.

During the walk to her house, Lacie thinks about her life. She is miserable at school. She likes art class and English class, but still being there day after day with her classmates is exhausting. She has always found it difficult to make friends. When she looks at people, she feels like they already know everything bad or embarrassing about her. They look at her with appalled expressions, judging her. She doesn't know how to defend herself from their scrutinizing eyes, so she just stares blankly forward, trying to get through the days with as little confrontation as possible.

Lacie doesn't spend much time inside her house either. It's an old house. The paint is chipping off the walls, like a snake shedding its skin. Everything also has a faint mildewy smell. The worst part of it, though, is the loneliness. She enters the house, throwing her backpack in a chair. Her mom shoots her a look.

"Dinner's not ready. Go upstairs and do your homework." She sits in her usual spot in the kitchen, wearing her usual clothes. A long floral housedress and slippers. She sits in the corner, by the window so that she can blow the smoke from her cigarette outside.

LITTLE FOXES

Lacie both resents and pities her mom. She has seen photos of her from when she was a younger woman, even from when she was Lacie's age. She used to be so happy looking. She wasn't necessarily drop-dead gorgeous, but her face bloomed with rosiness, and that gave her a beautiful quality.

The woman sitting before her now, however, is depleted of that former quality. She almost always holds a permanent frown on her face. Someone once told Lacie that it takes more effort to frown than it does to smile, and her first thought was that her mother must be very tired all the time then. Lacie also resents her because she used to be that blooming, happy person with her, when she was little. But that was a long time ago…before things changed.

She has fading memories of her mom singing and dancing around the house. Her dad would grab her mother by the waist. Then, her mom would pick up Lacie, pulling her into a giant bear hug that would send the three of them tumbling, and laughing, to the floor. But then, her dad disappeared from her life and her mom changed.

It didn't happen all at once. It was a slow thing, but it did happen, and Lacie can't help but think that maybe her mom just hates her and that's why she changed. Not too long after that, her mom re-married a man who does nothing but drink and zone out on the couch. Lacie knows he doesn't love her. She's not even sure if he actually loves her mom either. The two of them never express affection, at least not in front of her.

Lacie defiantly plops herself down on the couch, in her stepdad's spot, and turns on the TV. Her mom just sighs and continues smoking.

A little while later, her stepdad walks through the door. When he sees Lacie, he stops. For one brief, surreal moment, they just stare at one another.

"Get up."

"But…"

"GET UP," he howls. A ripple courses through the rickety house, like an earthquake, then settles again in an eerie silence.

Lacie feels shocked and betrayed by his outburst. His over-the-top response gives her the urge to act in kind, which is exactly what she does.

"I hate you," she yells as loud as she can and then stomps out through the front door.

Lacie sits on the porch for a little while, giving her parents ample time to come rushing out after her. They don't.

LITTLE FOXES

She sits between the wooden slats of the porch railing. Her toes brush the smooth earth, flattened by years of being trodden on, below her.

Her childlike impatience starts to kick in and she abandons the prospect of waiting around. She squeezes her skinny limbs through the slats and jumps down to the ground. As she does, she falls onto her knees.

She twists her body around, so that she can use the porch to pull herself up, but before she does, she sees something. There's a rotted section in the wood on the porch frame. It leaves a gaping hole, leading to the space underneath the porch. It is a hole she could probably fit through, with some finagling. She peers into the hole. It's black depth seems to know no bounds. It beckons her into it, like a siren call that she can't ignore.

It's dark. Only small traces of light creep in through cracks and other small holes. There is very little room to move. Lacie crawls forward on her belly, dragging her body across the dirty ground.

A tight gasp escapes her mouth when something, about three feet in front of her, shifts, then lets out a low, measured hiss.

Lacie stops moving and stays perfectly still, for what feels like hours. Her eyes eventually begin to adjust to the darkness, and she starts to make out the shape of an animal. It looks like a possum. She creeps forward a little more. The hissing starts again, but the animal doesn't run away. It just shifts itself a little unsteadily.

Lacie remembers the slim Jim she had shoved in her pocket at school, for later. She strenuously shifts her body so that she can reach her pocket. It's still there. She brings it up to her mouth and rips at the plastic with her teeth. Then she breaks off a piece of the meat stick and throws it towards the animal. It doesn't land close enough for it to reach.

"Dammit," she swears. She then tries again, this time tossing it more gracefully.

The animal hisses again, but, smelling the meat, it stretches its neck forward, sniffing. Once convinced that it's not a trap, it grabs the food and chews rapidly. While it's distracted, Lacie inches forward a bit more. That's when she notices that the front leg closest to her is nothing more than a bloodied stump. She stares, bewildered, at the dark congealed blood, where the foot should be. It's the first time she's ever seen such a horrific wound.

The animal, done with its piece of meat, grunts at her. She realizes that it must be starving, unable to move around with its injury. She breaks up the rest of the slim Jim and places it in front of the animal.

As it eats, hungrily, she whispers a promise. "Don't worry, I will come back tomorrow with more."

Chapter 66

Testimony of Dawn McCleary

"Please state your name for the record."

"Dawn Marie McCleary."

"And how did you know Michelle and Laura Fox?"

"They were my friends, well Michelle was my friend. We met in school, but I knew Laura, too. She hung out with us a lot."

"And who is us?"

"Me, Julie and Michelle."

"And, for the record, the Julie you are referring to is Julie Iverston?"

"Yes, back then her last name was Watson, but yes. We were inseparable at that age, but Michelle and Laura were also very close. They were…sorry. It's just difficult to talk about…. They were always together. It really was sweet."

Chapter 67

Testimony of Julie Iverston

"And how did you know Michelle and Laura Fox?"

"Michelle was my best friend. Laura was her little sister. She followed Michelle around like a lost puppy. At the time it annoyed me, but now…I just can't stop seeing those wide, bewildered eyes of hers every night when I go to sleep."

Chapter 68

Testimony of Dawn McCleary

"Tell me about Saturday, April 10th, 2004."

"It was the day before Easter. Michelle wanted to go to the mall to look at the Easter decorations. She was crafty and artistic. She would get super excited about that sort of thing…"

"After the girls went missing, you reported to police that there was a man staring at your group in the food court. Is that correct?"

"Yes…I wanted to tell an adult at the time, but Julie confronted him, and he went away, so it just didn't seem necessary."

Chapter 69

Testimony of Julie Iverston

"He looked like an animal. His eyes were glazed over and he was hyper focused on our table…on Michelle and Laura. He didn't even notice that I had approached him and was yelling at him at first. But, when he did, something shifted. It was like he suddenly realized that he was drawing attention to himself.

"He turned on his heel and walked away."

Chapter 70

Lacie crawls under the porch and breathes a sigh of relief when the possum is still there. It hisses at her when she starts to get close, but when she pulls the food out of her pocket and gently tosses it in front of the animal, it eats, hungrily, just as it did before.

With each bite, it becomes more and more distracted and Lacie inches closer and closer. Her fingertips throb with anticipation as she reaches her hand out towards the animal, wanting more than anything to pet it and love it with all she has in her.

In one brief, shining moment, she makes contact with its fur. It's dirty and matted, but soft and it's everything Lacie wanted and more. The moment, however, is fleeting.

In an instant, faster than Lacie could've thought possible, the possum's head jerks towards her. And then it bites her.

She pulls her hand back, as a reaction, but doesn't realize what has happened until she looks down and sees the blood. Before she can think about what she should do, the scream erupts from her mouth like a volcano, spewing burning lava everywhere.

Chapter 71

Testimony of Dawn McCleary

"Do you recognize this?"

"It looks like the sketch that the police officer drew, based on our description of the staring man at the mall."

"I'm going to show you an arrest photo. This is Lee Conrad's arrest photo, taken several years after the mall incident."

"Oh my god…That's him."

"Who is it?"

"The staring man from the mall. They look almost exactly the same."

Chapter 72

Testimony of Julie Iverston

"Would you say that you got a decent look at the staring man, from up close?"

"Yes, I was right in front of him."

"And is that man here in this court room today?"

"Yes, he is."

"Let the record show that the witness has pointed towards the defendant. Mrs. Iverston, it has been twenty years since that day. How are you so sure?"

"He may have aged, but his black eyes haven't changed at all."

Chapter 73

Lacie crawls out into the light outside the space under the porch. She continues to crawl on her stomach, until she runs into something…her stepfather's legs.

She looks up, but the setting sun shines bright above him, obscuring his face, making it look like he just emerged from a great ball of fire. She knows he's upset, though, because of the hands that grab her roughly and pull her to her feet, shaking her back and forth, like she's made of liquid.

Lacie looks down at the bite on her hand. Drops of red blood seep out and are shaken to the dusty earth below.

Maybe she is.

Later, that night, Lacie lays on her bed. Her cheeks are dry but streaked with old tears. She strokes the bandage on her hand, gingerly. Her mom took her to the hospital and the doctor said she had to get a rabies shot. It was a huge shot, and it was inserted into the fatty part of her backside, which is now throbbing with pain. Her stepfather didn't go. He was madder than Lacie had ever seen him in her life.

LITTLE FOXES

She thinks back to that brief encounter when she was caressing the possum's soft fur. It was all worth it.

Chapter 74

The next morning, Lacie walks outside, with a pocket full of food, ready to make up with her new friend. Instead, she sees her stepfather, on his hands and knees with a rake, pulling something out of the hole in the porch.

As the tuft of fur emerges from the hole, she also registers the pile of limp furry bodies outside the hole.

Her possum is laying belly-up with its tongue lolling out of one side of its open mouth. Its body is stiff and dried out, like the taxidermized deer that adorn the walls of her grandfather's house. And there are more, equally stiff, but smaller bodies, laying all around it.

Her possum was a mother.

Chapter 75

Testimony of Nancy Pritchard

An image projects onto a bright screen. It is the outside of a white house.

"Nancy, do you recognize this house?"

"Yes, I lived there for a time."

"Did you live there alone, or with someone else?"

"I was livin there with my boyfriend…Lee."

"And, just to clarify, Lee is the defendant- Lee Conrad?"

"Yes."

ADA Vivien Perez clicks a button on a remote control and the image on the screen changes.

"Is this a photo of the basement at that house, where you lived with Lee Conrad?"

"It's been a while…yes. I recognize the makeshift wall that made it two rooms."

Chapter 76

Testimony of Expert crime scene analyst, Dr. Herbert Schneider

The screen is now showing an image of a dark stain on a dingy carpet.

"Dr. Schneider, in your professional opinion, what is this stain?"

"It is blood."

"Objection."

"Sustained. Ms. Perez, please re-phrase."

"Dr. Schneider, you tested the sample collected from this stain, did you not?"

"I did."

"And what were your findings?"

"After careful testing, I concluded that there is a 99.98 percent chance that the stain is blood. Furthermore, there is a 97.9 percent chance that the blood belongs to Michelle Fox."

LITTLE FOXES

The image changes to one of a young girl with wispy, blonde hair. There are gaps in her wide smile where she is missing teeth.

"That's twelve-year-old, Michelle Fox, who went missing on Saturday, April 10th, 2004?"

"Yes, that's correct."

Chapter 77

Lacie sits, surrounded by tall grass, sketching a rabbit that is sitting five feet away. Her legs are beginning to fall asleep, so she stretches them out in front of her. The movement scares the rabbit, which lifts itself up on its haunches with its ears projected straight up in the air, before it takes off, hopping away into the distance faster than Lacie can blink.

"You have to force yourself to stay still and quiet."

Lacie, startled by the voice, turns and looks behind her. Lee is kneeling by a tree, about a few feet back. She has run into him a few times now in these woods. It's part of the reason she keeps coming back.

Lee saunters towards her and sits down. Lacie can feel his knee touching hers. It makes the heat rise to her face. She has never hung out with a boy, like for real. Let alone an older boy. She is not sure how to process the emotions that are churning within her. She's taken sex education at school, but the teacher just droned on, using boring words like fallopian tube and zygote. It was all very scientific. This…actually being so close to a boy that you can feel his hot breath on your skin. It's a very different thing, and it's confusing.

"Let me see that," he says.

Her hands are clammy as she hands him the sketchbook.

He holds it out in front of him, scrutinizing the page.

"It's good. You have talent." He rips the page from the book and folds it up neatly. Then he tucks it into his back pocket. "Do you want me to help you catch one?"

At first, Lacie is confused, but then she understands his question and a smile break across her face, like a wave.

"My own bunny-rabbit…like to keep?"

Chapter 78

Testimony of Nancy Pritchard

The image projected on the screen is of two young blonde girls. It looks like a first day of school photo. The girls stand, holding hands. The older one is smiling studiously at the camera, while the younger girl's nervous gaze is fixed upward, on her older sister.

"Have you ever seen these two girls?"

"Yeah…they were all over the TV after they went missing."

"Let me clarify. Have you ever seen them at the house that you lived in with Lee Conrad?"

Silence.

"Ms. Pritchard, might I remind you that you are under oath and that you must either answer the question or be held in contempt."

"They were there."

"When were they there?"

LITTLE FOXES

"It was a long time ago. They looked just like they did in that photo…"

"Was it in 2004?"

"Yes."

"Was it Easter weekend?"

"I think so."

"Can you please describe for the court what happened when they were there?"

"Nothin, really. Lee told me that he was watchin them for someone. He said I needed to make them eat. When I went down to the basement, they were holdin each other on the couch and crying, like they were dying. I've always been good with children. I tried to make them comfortable and happy. I even tried telling them a story, but they weren't havin it. They didn't thank me for the food I made for them and the little one even kicked me when I tried to wipe the dirt off her face."

"Did anyone else ever visit the house while the girls were there?"

"People came and went from time to time. I didn't keep track."

"And were these people male or female?"

"They were men, folks Lee knew."

"Nancy, did you ever ask Lee what was going to happen to the girls?"

"No. After a couple days, I went to stay with my sister for a few weeks. When I came back, they were gone."

Chapter 79

Lacie steadies her breath, just like he taught her. In…and out…in….and out. She looks through the binoculars he gave her. The rabbit is there. Just inches away from its hind leg is a rope, laying on the ground. Lee taught her how to make it. A proper snare. If the rabbit steps into it and then tries to run, the rope will tighten around its leg, holding it there, but only temporarily, until she releases it. And then she will make up for it by loving it forever.

As she lays on her stomach in the grass, she can feel his presence beside her- watching her. She doesn't dare look at him now, though, for fear that she will lose her focus.

The rabbit's body tenses. It perks up its ears and freezes. It remains that way for what feels like forever, before turning and hopping away, in the opposite direction. It's leg just barely misses the snare.

"Fuck, that was close", says Lee, sitting up beside her.

"So Fucking close", she exclaims. Saying the word feels like ripping off a band aide. Fast and a little scary. She doesn't normally use 'bad language', but she wants to seem older than she is in front of him.

LITTLE FOXES

Lacie crosses her legs over each other and re-ties her right shoelace, which had come undone. "Did I do anything wrong this time," she asks, still looking down at her shoe.

Lee reaches out and lifts her chin up. "You were perfect."

He rubs his thumb across the bottom of her chin briefly, before letting his arm drop. Then, he reaches into his pocket, pulling out a pack of cigarettes. He brings one to his lips, but then pauses and looks at her. "Do you want one?"

Lacie knows she shouldn't, but she finds herself nodding. She wants him to think she's cool."

He smiles as he leans in to light it for her. "Trust me, we'll get one…with time."

Chapter 80

Was that a knock at the door? Abby looks up at the clock on the wall. How long has she been sitting here? It was definitely a knock.

She gets up and walks to her apartment door, standing on her tiptoes to peer through the peep hole. No one is there, but on the ground, in front of her door, sits a brown paper bag.

Abby opens the door and quickly grabs the bag. She takes a deep breath, unsure of what she's about to see, and then she opens it and looks inside.

There are four items in the bag. A nirvana t-shirt, a pink toothbrush, a bottle of shampoo and a bottle of conditioner. They are the things she left at Oscar's apartment.

Anger wells up inside her. How dare he come here and terrorize her like that, out of the blue. She grabs the bag and runs out of her apartment, not even bothering to put on shoes. She's a fast runner, even with bare feet. She bolts across the courtyard in front of her apartment and into the open expanse of the parking lot. Then she spots him. He is fumbling with his keys, unlocking his car door.

LITTLE FOXES

Abby runs over to him and, when she gets close enough, she hurls the bag at him. It hits his car with a loud thud, leaving a dent in the back door, before sliding to the ground. The bag rips open and the shampoo bottle rolls out. It lands between them. Its runny pink contents seep out, spreading like a disease all over the parking lot. The strawberry aroma fills the air between them.

The smell, combined with the look on Oscar's face makes Abby momentarily re-think her actions. He's scared…of her. She has to say something, so she attacks. "Who do you think you are leaving a bag at my doorstep and then just dipping, without even so much as a phone call or a heads up, like some sort of creepy psycho stalker?"

Oscar's expression changes so instantly that Abby starts to wonder if he was ever actually afraid, or if she just imagined it. Now, his furrowed brow and the dark cloud over his features indicate only one emotion - anger. Nevertheless, when he speaks, his voice is even and controlled. "I have called you, several times in fact. You've completely stopped answering my calls and texts."

Abby pulls her phone from her pocket and looks at the blank screen. She presses in the power button, but it's no use. The battery is dead. How long has it been that way?

"I actually thought for a while that you might be dead in a ditch somewhere, but then your mom told me that you were fine."

LITTLE FOXES

"Well since you're so chummy with my mom, maybe the two of you should just go fuck each other," she retorts.

Oscar looks stricken. As though she just slapped him across the face. He takes two long strides towards her, bridging the gap between them, so that he glares down at her. "For the record, I didn't reach out to your mom first, she reached out to me. And that's because she was worried…about you. Is that why you researched my mother, who I never told you about, lied your way into her holding facility and then harassed a fragile woman with dementia?"

"Yes," Abby retorts. I was worried too. I was downright afraid for my own well-being."

Oscar lets out a breath and backs up, just a little. It's enough, though, to make her feel like she has the upper hand.

"How did you know about my closet? Did you stumble upon it accidentally? And once you figured out my secret, what was your endgame with the cryptic letters and the photo and the newspaper clipping? Or do you just get off on threatening women?"

His expression changes into something Abby did not expect-confusion. It dawns on her that she has greatly mis-calculated the situation.

"Abby… I…don't know."

LITTLE FOXES

Before he can finish, she turns and runs away. Back across the parking lot, cutting through the courtyard, into her apartment. She falls into her bed, wrapping the covers around her face.

And she screams.

Chapter 81

Testimony of Retired Detective, Mark Davis

"Were you present at the time that the blood was found?"

"Yes, I was."

"And can you tell the court where it was found."

"It was found in the basement of the house that was Lee Conrad's residence, at the time of the Fox sisters' disappearance."

"Can you please describe the basement for us?"

"It looked like it had originally been one open room, but someone, presumably Lee, had installed a makeshift wall, separating it into a larger section and a smaller section. The larger section had carpeting, which according to the current resident, had not been changed since Lee moved out. In Lee's own words, there was a couch in this section. That is where his ex-girlfriend, Nancy, saw the sisters. We believe this section is where Michelle was kept most of the time…within proximity to the couch…"

LITTLE FOXES

"Objection. Without a body, there is no physical evidence of sexual assault."

"Your honor, In Lee's own interviews, he provides eye-witness testimony that Michelle was assaulted, sexually."

"I'll allow it to stand on the record, but Let's keep the conjecture to a minimum."

"Thank you, your honor. Mark, was the couch still present when you investigated the basement?"

"No, unfortunately, the current resident claimed it had a foul odor, so she got rid of it. But as I mentioned the carpet was still there. And that is where we found Michelle Fox's blood."

"And what about Laura Fox. Is there any evidence that she was there as well?"

"According to both Nancy and Lee, Laura was a little less…compliant. We believe for that reason that she was kept in the smaller room most of the time. This room was essentially a cold dungeon. There was no light and no carpeting. We did, however find a handprint on the wall."

"Which wall?"

"The one that was added. The one that faced out to the rest of the room."

"Were you able to identify who this handprint may have belonged to?"

"Yes…the third-grade class she was in had just studied fingerprinting that year…it belonged to Laura Fox."

"And can you tell the court where Lee Conrad was residing when you began to interview him in respect to the disappearance of the Fox sisters?"

"He was 'residing' in Delaware state prison…for raping a fifteen-year-old girl."

"What vehicle did Lee own at the time of his arrest?"

"It was a white, Ford contractor van. There were no seats or windows in the back and…he had rigged the manual locks so that they didn't work. You needed the key fob in order to open the doors from the inside.

Chapter 82

"He-llooo? Earth to Lacie!"

Lacie is drawn back to reality by his voice. She lets her eyes re-focus. On her lap, sits a cumbersome pile of clover flowers, all tied together in a long chain. Lee, who is sitting across from her in the grass, nudges her shoe with his own.

"I thought I'd lost you there," he says, with a slightly obnoxious grin.

Lacie looks at his face. Really looks. Acne scars line the ridge of his jaw. His nose is thick and a little crooked, at the bridge. His hair, which is starting to break past his shoulders, lies greasy and limp, like it hasn't been washed in ages.

She doesn't know why she keeps being drawn to this place. To him. Part of her is repelled by him, disgusted even. Alarm bells go off in her brain every time she's with him, screaming that this isn't right. That she should run away as fast as she can. But then there's something that brings her back. Makes her blush when he looks at her. Whispers to her soul, or whatever's inside. She's so lonely and he's the only person who talks to her. More than that, he listens and doesn't lie to her. He treats her like an adult.

"Sorry," says Lacie. "I just had a crappy day at school."

"Missy Briggs?" He says the name in a high-pitched, mock-valley-girl voice.

Lacie laughs despite herself. "Yes. She always has to draw attention to my dirty shoes and clothes, in front of everyone." She covers one of her shoes with the other. She knows that Lee's worn brown boots are even dirtier than her own, but she still feels embarrassed saying the words in front of him, for some reason.

Lee picks up his knife and a piece of wood that he's been sharpening to a point for days now. The sharp blade glints as he slides it across the wood, effortlessly shaving off the rough pieces, revealing the smooth, amber-white wood underneath.

"You know, I think it's about time someone taught that girl a lesson."

Chapter 83

The white egg glistens in the dusky glow of the setting sun. It makes a light whistle noise as it peels through the air around it, like a torpedo. Then, it makes contact with a window, shattering against the glass. Egg juices drip slowly towards the ground, succumbing to the inevitability of gravity.

"Damn! Nice shot!"

Lee's voice breaks Lacie from her reflective thoughts. She looks down at her hand in disbelief. Is she actually egging Missy's house right now? The excitement from doing something risky and totally out of character buzzes across her skin, like an electric current.

Lacie leans down to pick up another egg. Just as she raises her arm to throw it, the front door of the house opens. A man steps out onto the front porch. He has a rolled-up newspaper in his hand and he waves it at them while making incoherent noises and gesticulating wildly.

Lacie and Lee both take off running. Lacie feels light as she runs. It feels as though any moment her feet will lift off the ground and she will glide effortlessly away.

Lee reaches his arm towards her, and they hold hands, flying away together.

Chapter 84

Testimony of Brian Conrad

"You live in Clinchport, Virginia, is that correct?"

"Yes, mam. Me and my wife, May."

"And how many acres are included in that property?"

"Somewhere around fifteen."

"And do you often burn bonfires on this property?"

"Yeah, we got a good little spot set up. It gets chilly at night, even in the spring and summer. So, we light the bonfire and drink beer – it's what everyone does there."

"What relationship do you have with the defendant, Lee Conrad?"

"Well, he's my cousin, so he's kin."

"Did Lee visit you at this property during the summer of 2004?"

"Yes, mam."

"Did he let you know beforehand that he would be coming to visit?"

"He called me a few hours before he got there. I think he was calling from a payphone."

"Did he ask you to do anything for him before he arrived?"

"Yes, mam…he asked me to start the bonfire and get it goin nice and good."

"Did he say why?"

"He just said he was bringin something that needed burnin."

Chapter 85

Lacie walks towards the school bus with her head down, as usual. All of a sudden, she feels a sharp pain in her leg and then the air shifts around her. For a moment, it's as though she can feel the earth spinning. Then she's on her hands and knees on the rough cement and there are three sets of legs surrounding her.

She reaches for her bookbag, which has fallen to the ground beside her. Before she can grab it though, a foot- clad in perfectly pristine white Etnies, with pink accents- kicks it away from her grasping hands.

Lacie knows those shoes. She has admired and coveted them from afar many times. She knows they belong to Missy Briggs, but she looks up anyway. The sun burns in her eyes and obscures Missy's face, but her shiny brown hair encompasses her head like a mane and her scent wafts down, filling Lacie's senses with the essence of strawberry lip smackers.

"You think your little stunt last night with your homeless friend was funny. Only someone as deranged as you would make friends with a total creepster like that. My parents say it's because your father is a drunk who treats you and your mom like shit. I think you and I both know that it's just because you're a loser, though."

With those words, Missy and her two sidekicks walk away. Even if she had been able to think of a snappy comeback, they wouldn't have given her a chance to respond.

Chapter 86

The rain pelts down on Lacie. Her bike tires skid and struggle to keep straight as they glide through the large puddles that are forming on the road beneath them. Lacie is shivering violently and finds it difficult to steer, or even see what's ahead of her. She keeps going, though, until she reaches the spot in the road where she first saw him.

He is not there, of course, although part of her for some reason thought he might be. She doesn't know what to do. She can't seem to gain control of all the emotions that are swirling around in her head, pushing her forward, towards what? She doesn't know, but she can't stop herself. She flings herself off the bike, letting it drop at the side of the road. Then she runs.

She runs through the trees in the woods, where they have spent so much time together the past few weeks. The trees block most of the rain but the leaves and twigs on the ground are slick underneath her feet and she skids and lands on her hands and knees. The pain from the scratches that are there, from falling on the cement earlier, surges through her body and fuels her on. She runs blindly, as if guided by some invisible force. After a while, she doesn't even recognize where she is anymore, but she keeps moving forward.

Then, she sees it. The van that she saw on that first day. The one she has tried to imagine what is like on the inside several times since. It is at the edge of a small clearing and the trees are parted around it, so that the ominous clouds penetrate down onto it and surround it in terrible darkness.

A weird feeling begins to brew in Lacie's gut. What is she doing here? She stops and stills, ready to turn around and run back to her house- to her bed, but, there, sitting in the back of the van with the doors flung open, enjoying the darkness, is Lee. He had seen her and now it's too late.

Chapter 87

Testimony of May Conrad

"Do you remember Lee Conrad's visit to your home during the summer of 2004?"

"Yes, I recall it."

"Were there any suspicious circumstances about this visit?'

"Objection, Leading"

"Withdrawn. Mrs. Conrad, do you remember the defendant, Lee Conrad having a duffel bag in his possession during this visit?"

"Yes. It stunk something awful."

"Did you ask him what was in the bag?"

"Yeah, I wanted to know what that stench was. He said one of his dogs had died and he needed to burn it."

"Why did he need to come all the way to your house to burn it. Why not burn it where he lived?"

LITTLE FOXES

"He said his landlady had already gotten on him about burning stuff and he didn't want to deal with her."

"Did you ever see what was in the bag?"

"No…why would I?"

"How did Lee burn the contents of the bag without you seeing what was inside?"

"Well…he just threw the whole bag on the bonfire. I did think it was a little weird that he didn't want to keep the bag…but then again, that smell probably never woulda come out."

"How long did Lee keep the bonfire burning?"

"He was very persistent about keeping it goin through the night and even into the next day and night. The smell was so terrible, it changed the air. Our neighbors still complain about that stupid bonfire."

Chapter 88

Lacie sits inside the van. She is sitting towards the back end, by the doors, but she is sitting with her back to the wall and her knees pulled up in front of her. Lee sits on the opposite side, letting his legs hang out of the open doors.

She sips from the mug that he gave her, after convincing her to tell him about what happened with Missy and the other girls at school. Lacie could tell right away, from the smell, that it was alcohol. She had always been curious about why grownups drank so much of the stuff when it smelled so bad, but…now, sitting here listening to the rain while the alcohol burns the back of her throat and makes her feel numb…she thinks she gets it.

She looks around the van. There are no seats in the back. It is just one big, open space. There is, however, an old looking chair in one corner and a rolled up sleeping bag, along with a duffel bag with clothes spilling out of the top. Taped to the wall, across from where Lacie sits, is the picture she drew of the rabbit.

She studies the soft strokes of its fur and its calm posture. It is in its element, save for one ear, which is perched in an upward alert position- as if it knows something that the rest of the animal hasn't figured out yet.

As the night slowly grows darker, Lacie feels heavier. The lines of the drawing start to blur together and she struggles to even hold her head upright. The mug falls from her hand, which can't seem to grip things anymore. She laughs a little as she tries to make a fist, but instead her hand just flops around in front of her.

The smile disappears from her lips, however, when she sees him sliding towards her, silently. His face… has changed.

Chapter 89

Summer 2004

Hearing the car coming up behind him, Lee automatically extends his arm, thumb projected upwards. He doesn't actually expect anyone to stop, but he is relieved when the old, brown station wagon pulls over on the side of the road ahead of him.

"You can go ahead and throw your duffel there in the back, friend."

Lee eyes the bag, unsure, but then he places it, very carefully down in the back cab. When he seats himself in the front passenger seat, the aging man behind the wheel introduces himself as Carl. His eyes are weary, crow's feet reaching out from the corners like a disease that's spreading. But they are also kind.

"Where you headed, stranger," asks Carl.

"Up north- Clinchport."

"Well, that's kinda out there, but I am headed in that general direction. I can probably get you within about six miles, or so."

Lee nods and glances nervously behind him.

LITTLE FOXES

"What's bringin you all the way out to those parts?"

"I have family out there."

"Ah, I see…" The man's face changes as he sniffs the air, like a dog. "I don't mean to be rude, fella, but your bag back there smells…like death."

Lee smiles. He expected this. "Yeah, you know, like I said I'm visiting my family, and I got all this meat, for barbequing, at a real good deal. Bought it from this guy that's friends with my cousin. Guy told me it was real fresh, so I set out, thinkin it'd be okay, but damn it, I think he maya lied to me about that."

"Oh, I definitely think he did, that meat has gone off," says Carl, holding his hand over his nose.

About forty minutes later, Lee exits the station wagon, a good five miles sooner than Carl had originally promised, but it doesn't matter. He'd rather be alone anyway. Lee sets off again on foot.

He thinks about what he needs to do when he gets there. His cousin, Brian, will have the bonfire goin. He will put the bag on the fire and make sure that it keeps goin until the whole thing is burned. Ashes to ashes…

Chapter 90

Testimony of Retired Detective, Mark Davis

"You were present for the property search of Brian and May Conrad, were you not?"

"Yes. We searched the entire property, but specifically focused on where the bonfire was set up."

"And what was the result of that search?"

"We found some bone fragments and …a part of a handmade bracelet."

Vivien Perez presses a button on a remote and the projector screen bursts to life, displaying an image of small, white pieces of bone and teeth laying on a table.

"Are these the bone fragments that were discovered?"

"Yes."

LITTLE FOXES

She clicks the button again, changing the image to one of a charred piece of woven fabric. The colorful intertwining threads are visible, even through the fire damage.

"And this is the bracelet?"

"Yes."

"Did you have a suspicion as to who this bracelet may have belonged to?"

"Yes…aahh, sorry…we sent if off for testing, along with the bone fragments, but we were pretty certain it had belonged to Laura Fox."

"I know this is difficult, but could you please explain to the court how you came to that conclusion?"

"The girls' parents identified it. They said that Michelle had made it and given it to Laura as a gift and that she never took it off. They also gave us a photo of her wearing it."

Click. The image once again changes to one of Laura Fox. She is about nine or ten. Her cheeks are flushed, and she is in an action pose. Her hands are poised above her head and her feet are spread apart- readying herself for a cartwheel. On her raised right arm, there is a bracelet made of multi-colored threads, woven together.

Chapter 91

Her other senses return first, before she can open her eyes. The overwhelming acrid smell of sweat is the first thing that pulls her back to reality. She thinks it's partly her own, but also someone else's.

The second thing is movement. Her body is moving back and forth. Lacie feels like she is laying face up on a trampoline, with someone jumping all around her. She tries to hold onto that thought, imagining that it's a warm summer day. The sun is kissing her face with its warmth and, as she looks lazily to the side, her mother's dainty feet make contact with the taut vinyl and then lift off- remaining suspended in the air for what feels like forever, before coming back down and once again shaking her equilibrium.

It's a nice thought, but she feels it slipping away like a dream when the pain sets in. Lacie opens her eyes. It's him. He is on top of her. His features are hard and his face is twisted into stern concentration. His shoulder length hair is wet, with sweat. It drips onto her face and neck as he writhes back and forth, shaking her whole body.

LITTLE FOXES

Her skin rubs against the brittle carpet below her. That's when she realizes that her arms are no longer tied. She closes her eyes again. She needs to get through this.

Chapter 92

Lacie crawls forward. It's dark in here, but light filters in through the multi-colored blankets all around her. It's like being inside a soft prism…and she loves it.

"Lacie, where aaaarree you?" Her mother's voice echoes through the space. She doesn't sound very far.

Lacie takes off- moving forward on her hands and knees, like her life depends on it. Panic and elation both well up inside her chubby, four- year- old limbs, pushing her onward. It bubbles over and bursts out of her in the form of a giggle. But then, she realizes she is all alone and panic sets in. She starts to cry.

Just then, a blanket to her right starts moving towards her. The shape of arms reaches through it, grabbing her and pulling her upwards. The soft warmth of the blanket envelops her. Then, the cloth is pulled away from her face and there is the face of her mother- staring down at her, radiating love.

Chapter 93

Moments later, the movement stops. Lee lets out a low grunt and then rolls off Lacie, onto the floor beside her. Lacie is relieved, but she does not dare move yet.

Lee rolls onto his side, with his face turned away from Lacie. After a while, she starts to think he has fallen asleep, but then she hears a quiet sobbing. It penetrates the stillness of the van. Lacie closes her eyes shut as tightly as she can. It is difficult to lay there and listen to his pain, when all she can think about is her own and how all she wants to do right now is cry too, but she still does not dare make a noise.

Lacie lays there like that for what seems like hours. Waiting and listening. Every sense in her body is hyper-aware, except her sense of touch. Her legs and arms are beginning to go numb from the lack of movement, but she continues to wait.

Finally, a low snore emanates from Lee's body. Lacie turns her head, very slowly and quietly, towards him. His face is still turned away from her, but he seems to be asleep.

This has got to be it. She needs to move.

LITTLE FOXES

She forces herself upward, to a seated position. Every cell in her body is screaming pain, but she has to push it away so that she can focus on getting out of here. She pulls up her pants, which were gathered around her ankles. Then, she moves onto her hands and knees.

Crumbs scrape against the palms of her hands as she pushes herself forward, silently. One inch at a time. The urge to look at him is strong, but she keeps her eyes on the back doors. They are still cracked open slightly. A streak of moonlight creeps in, like a beacon in the dark.

When she finally makes it there, she breathes in a silent sigh of relief, but then pauses. She pulls her legs underneath her so that she is perched in a crouching position. It occurs to her that once she opens the door, there is a good chance he might wake up. She takes a few deep inhales and exhales, trying to steady her emotions. Then she finds the door handle and pushes it open.

The cool night breeze trickles in. It caresses her face and bare arms, and her brain goes numb. The thinking part is over, now is the time for action. She jumps down.

"Lacie?" The word catches her ears the same second as her feet touch the ground. It is soft and pleading.

Lacie runs. The wind whips around her, whistling in her ear. She lets her legs take over. For a little while, she imagines she is actually flying, instead of running, but the illusion is broken when her foot catches on a large tree root, sticking out of the ground.

When she hits the ground, pain surges through her left arm. It doesn't make any sense to Lacie. Why does her arm hurt and not her foot? She forces herself to stand and continue forward. She can't stop now.

A moment later, she can start to make out the road through the trees. As she breaks out of the forest and onto the gravelly side of the road, she lets out a long sigh of relief. She recognizes her surroundings. She is near her bus stop- and close to home.

Before setting off again, she looks down for the first time and realizes that she has no shoes on. Her feet are swollen and bloody. As she looks down at them in shock, blood drips onto her toes from above. It takes her a moment to realize that it's coming from her arm.

There is an open gash in her left arm. It is bleeding profusely. She must've caught it on the tree root when she fell. Her first instinct is to laugh, but then her brain seems to catch up and the laugh transforms into a sob before it's even finished. After the first one escapes, the sobs start pouring out of her like a flood.

She can't seem to control it, so she just lets it happen. She sobs as she crosses the road. Just as she makes it to the other side, she starts to see headlights coming around the corner. She ducks into the forest, just off the path to her house. She has played in this forest so many times. She knows each and every tree, they are imprinted in her mind like the faces of the people she loves.

The vehicle begins to turn the corner and comes into view. Is that a van? Is it slowing down? Lacie starts to feel very woozy- like she is going to faint. She moves to a little copse of trees and thornbushes nearby. There is a child-sized hole at the bottom. She pushes her pre-teen body through the hole for the first time in years.

Inside, it's like being alone in a fairytale. The thick vines of the thornbushes keep the inside secluded- cut off from the world. Lacie lies down.

Memories flood her brain of simpler times. She would spend hours in this very spot as a young child. Sometimes she was a witch, brewing up potions. Sometimes she was a forest troll, making dinner for her troll children. Sometimes she would lay on her belly, pretending she was a sniper. She would aim a long stick, perched in her arms, which served as her rifle, at nearby birds, pretending they were enemy soldiers. Other times, she just sat, listening to the rain. Her vision is blurry, and her mind is giving up. She listens to the soft sounds of nature, enveloping her, like a cocoon. Warmth blooms throughout her body and for the first time she feels safe. Then…she falls asleep.

Chapter 94

Lacie feels warm. It's as if someone is tucking her into a warm fleece blanket. Then they stroke her hair gently and kiss her lightly on the cheek before whispering, I love you.

Those words linger in her ears like a lost memory as she wakes. The harshness of reality sets in however, as she sits up. She is still outside in her hiding place. She picks the dewy leaves from her face. Her throat is extremely dry, and a deep pain emanates from her arm. She inspects the cut. It's covered in dried blood, but at least it's not still actively bleeding.

At first, relief floods through her when she realizes that Lee never came looking for her, or at least he never found her. As she carefully maneuvers through the woods to her house, though, relief begins to turn into a burning shame. She ran to him for comfort and deep down she must've known what he would do, right? This is all her fault. She can never tell anyone.

Chapter 95

Testimony of Expert crime scene analyst, Dr. Herbert Schneider

"When you analyzed the bracelet found at the Conrad property, what did you discover?"

"I discovered skin cells on the bracelet. When tested, they were a match for Laura Fox."

Chapter 96

Testimony of Janice Firestone

"Janice, please tell the court how old you were in early 2004."

"I was sixteen."

"And is that when you met the defendant?"

"Yes. I was an employee at the orange bowl."

"Where was the Orange Bowl that you worked at located?"

"It was inside the Turner Hill Mall."

"And how did you meet Lee Conrad?"

"He used to come by and order food during my shifts. He said he worked at the mall as a plainclothes security guard. It was his job to catch people who were stealing."

"How often did you see him there?"

"Well, I worked Friday, Saturday and Sunday evenings. He was usually there all three days."

LITTLE FOXES

"Tell me what happened on February 2nd, 2004."

"We had gotten accustomed to smoking outside together. He would give me cigarettes. On that day he…he pulled a knife out of his pocket. At first, I just thought he was showing off- he was like that. But, when I looked at his face, he was serious. His eyes were…black. I was scared."

"What happened next?"

"He put his arm around my waist, but held the knife real close against my side, so that I could feel the tip of it digging into my side. Then, he led me to the parking lot and forced me into the passenger seat of his van."

"Then what?"

"As soon as he shut my door, I started trying to open it, but it was locked. I tried the buttons, but they wouldn't work either. I felt trapped and I started to panic. When he got into the driver's side, my panic went into overdrive. I just started pushing and pressing buttons like crazy. That's when I realized the window worked, but it would only go down about halfway. Fortunately, I was much smaller back then. I didn't even think about it. I just jumped through that window and then ran back into the mall. I finished my shift. It was ridiculous, but I was in shock, and I didn't know what else to do, but I never went back. I quit the next day."

Chapter 97

Lacie had to get stitches in her arm. She told her mom she tripped in the woods, which wasn't really a lie. The doctor said that because it wasn't treated immediately, there will definitely be a scar. Just what she needs – a freakish scar for people to gawk at and ridicule her for.

Yesterday, two policemen showed up at their house. They were returning her bike, which was recovered from a van involved in a drunk driving fender bender. Apparently, they recovered some other items from the van as well and they suspected they were all stolen.

It took all her courage to ask them what happened to the driver – the man who'd been haunting her nightmares for the past few weeks. They said that he was arrested for drunk driving and theft, but that he posted bail and that he was probably planning on skipping town.

Those words are a huge relief to Lacie. She was scared to leave the house – worried she will run into him. Her stepfather was very upset that she let her bike get stolen. He yelled at and grounded her, after the policemen left.

It's okay though. Being grounded suits her. She doesn't feel like leaving or doing anything these days, anyway.

Chapter 98

Testimony of Elizabeth Kim

"Elizabeth, please tell the court how old you were in early 2004."

"I was twelve years old, almost thirteen. My Birthday is in June."

"Please tell us what happened on March 6th, 2004- when you were twelve."

"I was at the Turner Hill Mall with my mom and my little brother, John. We were shopping for church shoes- since Easter was coming up."

"Is that when you encountered the defendant?"

"Yes. We were in Sears, which was a huge store. My brother and I had wandered away from our mom. I was in the makeup department, pretending I was older and that I knew what it all was for. My brother was in the toy department, which was only a few aisles away.

After about ten minutes, I figured I'd better check on him, but I was stopped by a man- that man."

LITTLE FOXES

"Let the record show that Elizabeth has pointed to the defendant. Go on, Elizabeth, what happened after he stopped you?"

"He was holding a toy. It was a dinosaur. He told me that he had just caught my brother trying to steal the toy. He said he needed me to come outside to the parking lot so that he could question me. He also said he didn't want to get us in trouble and that if I did what he said everything would be okay."

"How did you react to that?"

"I was scared. I was a kid. I didn't really have a reason to disbelieve him, but it just didn't feel right. My mom had made it very clear that I shouldn't go anywhere with strangers, so I told him I needed to ask her first. He didn't like that, though. He started to get angry, asking me if I wanted to go to jail for helping my brother steal. I started to get scared then and I called out for my brother, as loud as I could. I could hear my brother running up behind us, so I turned to explain what was happening.

When I turned back towards the man, he had disappeared."

Chapter 99

Lacie stares at the pregnancy test again and then back at the instructions. She reads them for the fourth time, trying to figure out how to change the result. She needs it to say something different. Every time she reads it, though, it comes out the same. She is pregnant.

Chapter 100

Testimony of Maggie Porter

"Maggie, please tell the court when and how you met the defendant, Mr. Conrad."

"Well, it was around 2009 or 2010. I was a waitress at a diner, and he used to come in. He'd always order the plain burger and a banana milkshake, no matter what time of day it was."

"And when did the two of you become involved with one another?"

"Oh, it was pretty quick…a month or so after we met. He was just so kind to me….in those days."

"Did he eventually become unkind to you?"

"Yeah…a few months in he started having dark moods, that's what I called them. He would just become sullen and easily angered. He could be very unkind during those times."

"Where were you living in the late summer of 2010?"

LITTLE FOXES

"We were living together. He had convinced me to move to Fort Worth- in Texas. It was the first time I'd ever lived out west. That was when things started to get really bad."

"Bad, how?"

"I got pregnant. He was very angry when I told him. He screamed at me and punched a hole in our wall. Then he just disappeared for about a week. When he came back, he seemed a little better, though, so I stayed. And that just became our normal way of living. He would have an angry outburst. Then, he would leave for days at a time. Then, he would come back all calm and zen-like."

Things just continued like that for a while, until, one day, out of the blue, he wanted us to up and move to Delaware. It was strange how sudden it was, but my family lives in West Virginia, so I was happy to be closer to them, with the baby coming and all."

"And how were things after you moved to Delaware?"

"At first things were good- normal even. But, after a while his dark moods started up again. He told me he'd gotten a contracting job at this rich person's house and that he might be gone a lot.

He was, but honestly, I didn't mind so much anymore. One day, I was at work- I was workin at a laundry mat at that time- but I was havin some serious indigestion and stomach cramping. I was around

LITTLE FOXES

six or seven months pregnant at this time, so my boss said I should go home and rest."

"What happened when you got home?"

Well, first of all, I was surprised to see Lee's van parked in the back alley behind our apartment. It was kind of hidden, but I had to walk home from the bus stop and there was a shortcut that led to that back alley. I knew something was off the minute I walked through the door. The air was just very still, but I kept moving forward- like I was in a dream."

"And what did you see?"

"In the bedroom, I saw…Lee, standing beside the bed…having sex…but not really, because she wasn't moving. At first I thought…. I thought she might be dead. But then…her eyes fluttered open, and she looked right at me. It was then that I realized she was only a child.

I'm sorry, this is just bringing up a lot of bad stuff for me."

"It's okay, Maggie. Just take your time and tell us what happened next."

"Okay, so…after that it was kind of a blur. Everything happened so fast. When Lee noticed me standin there, his face was all twisted in rage. I aint never seen a face like that before, or since. My first reaction was to beg him to forgive me, so that he wouldn't hurt me, but…something about that little girl's face, or maybe it was that I was pregnant. I don't know, but I just wanted to help her."

"What did you do?"

"I didn't have a cell phone at that time, so I ran to the kitchen to call 911. When he came in and saw me on the phone, tellin em what happened he just… lost it. He grabbed me and slammed me down on the floor. Then, he just started punching and kicking me. Over and over. After a while I just passed out.

When I woke up, I was in the hospital. They told me that the cops had to pull him off me to arrest him. They said the girl was safe, with her family.

They also told me that I went into labor from the stress and all. And that…my baby had died."

Chapter 101

She sits in the cold waiting room. She looks down at the pamphlet that someone had shoved into her hand outside, in the parking lot. There is a picture of a fetus on the front. The caption reads, shouldn't all human beings…have human rights? She stares at it, trying to make sense of her jumbled emotions. She can feel the tears starting to form in her eyes.

A hand, her mother's, reaches over and grabs a hold of her own. They don't look at each other, they just sit like that for a long time. Until a nurse enters the room and calls her name.

Chapter 102

Light begins to filter in with the darkness, creating shapes of muted color. The soft melody of fifties music- the stuff her mom likes- trickles in from somewhere beyond the door of her room. There is also the smell of something strong and chemically, bleach or ammonia.

Abby sits up, groggily. She squints at the sunlight streaming in through the window, as her eyes adjust to her surroundings. She's in her bed. But not just in it, but like tucked into it, like a child. Her room also seems very…tidy. The open curtains, letting in the outside elements, cinch it in her mind that this is all someone else's doing…her mom.

She finds her mom in the kitchen, cleaning. The spray bottle in her hand makes a repeated squeaking sound every time she furiously squeezes the trigger. "Well, it's good to know you're alive," she says, as if it's just a normal day and Abby is her useless teenage daughter who can't survive without her.

LITTLE FOXES

"What are you doing here?" Abby's voice is a hoarse whisper. She suddenly has a flashback of scream-crying into her pillow. She automatically begins preparing the coffee maker.

"You called me. You were very upset and not making any sense, so I came over. And it's a good thing I did because this place is a mess." She gestures towards the living room with her arm but continues scrubbing the same spot on the kitchen counter."

Abby can't remember much from last night…or maybe even from the last few nights. It certainly wouldn't be the first time she's called her mom, upset about something. Abby cradles her mug of coffee, fresh from the pot and sips it slowly, letting it soothe her sore throat. She leans against the counter, staring blankly at the living room before her.

Abby feels disconnected to it all- like it's a part of someone else's life and she's just a bystander drinking coffee. She pulls out her phone and starts scrolling through the mountain of missed calls and un-replied to messages. Then, she checks her outgoing calls. She might need to do damage control.

Something is off, though. She looks blankly at the screen, trying to make it make sense. There are multiple out-going calls to restaurants that deliver near her. Chinese, pizza, Mexican food- some made within minutes of each other. That is not what concerns her the most, though. There is no call made to her mom. She scrolls through everything from the last three days. She did not call her mom…so why is she really here?

Abby turns suddenly and faces her mother, who is chatting away incessantly. "Why are you here," she demands.

"Wh…what do you mean? I told you I'm here because you called, and I was worried." Her mother grabs the broom, perched against the counter and begins to sweep.

Abby grabs the broom handle and grounds herself, holding a firm stance so that her mother cannot move. She holds out her phone with her other hand, facing the call-log screen towards her mother. "Why…are…you…here?"

Her mother lets go of the handle- her expression changing to one of defeat and fear. She shrugs dismissively. "Okay, so you didn't call me…but I actually did come because I was worried. You were clearly spiraling and I thought maybe I could intervene and stop it this time."

"What does that mean? How did you know I was spiraling?"

Her mother pulls the fake house plant on the kitchen counter towards her. She pushes back the leaves to reveal a small black box. "I saw you."

LITTLE FOXES

"You've been spying on me," Abby yells.

"For your own good," retorts her mother. "When you started spouting nonsense about threatening messages, I knew it was happening again. I thought I could stop it this time before it got too bad.

Abby is stunned. "What are you talking about?"

"There. That's another sign. You've done this before, sweetheart. Driving around all hours of the night. Sending yourself threats and then blaming someone else. Trashing your apartment and living like…an animal. I just don't know what to do. You always forget about the past when you are spiraling again."

Abby looks around her and sees her apartment for the first time in weeks. It is wrecked. It does look like a wild animal has been living there. Papers and mail are strewn everywhere, along with open food containers of half-eaten take out. Abby investigates an open carton of Chinese food and recoils when she sees maggots crawling around at the bottom. There are piles of clothes here and there that look as though they've been slept on. The trash can has been turned over in the middle of the floor, flies swirl around its contents.

All of this should persuade Abby that her mother is right, but it only makes her angrier. Also, what does she mean 'she forgets about the past'? The past is ALL she can think about. It consumes every waking moment of her existence, like a fire that never dies.

"I haven't forgotten about my dad, even though you tried to take his memory away from me."

Abby's mother is stunned. "I just…it was hard for me…your father, he suffered. He was depressed a lot towards the end, and we were fighting, but I still loved him so much.

Then, he killed himself. He abandoned us. And…quite frankly, I saw that dark sadness in you too…and I wanted to erase it."

Abby is shocked. She had pieced together years ago that her father was dead, but she never knew that he took his own life.

"You're a liar."

"Abby, I'm not ly-"

"GET OUT, YOU LYING BITCH!"

Chapter 103

Lacie sits on the small bed, which has been hers for the past three months. She looks around the sparse room. There is another single bed on the other side of the room, which had belonged to Millie. She was nice, well as nice as a person who's totally bonkers can be. She checked out a couple weeks ago, but before she left, she told Lacie that she would definitely be back the next time she was forced to spend time with her mother-in-law. "You'd think they'd learn," she had said. "Next time, I might not just hurt myself."

Lacie stares at the wall across from her bed. The whole thing is covered from ceiling to floor with a wallpapered forest landscape. For some reason, it has a calming effect on her. She looks deep into the dark reaches beyond the trees, wondering what is lurking in there. Absentmindedly, she traces the track marks on her arms, which are starting to fade.

Claire, the receptionist, appears at the door. "It's time to go, hon." Lacie stands, throwing her bag over her shoulder, and walks somberly out of the room. At the end of the hall, she stops, waiting for Claire to swipe her key card, buzzing open the double doors looming before her. Claire pauses and turns to her, then pulls her into a warm hug.

LITTLE FOXES

"This is it hon. You're free." She moves back, putting her hands on Lacie's shoulders and looks into her eyes. "You got this, okay?"

Lacie fights the tears that are threatening to come. All she can muster in response is a quick, yet grateful nod. And then, the doors buzz loudly and swing open. The light from the lobby leaks into the quiet hallway, infecting it with life on the outside. Then, Claire steps forward, beckoning Lacie to follow, and just like that, she's a part of the outside world and her time spent locked away from polite society over the last three months, is already becoming a far off memory, like a dream.

Lacie's mother greets her at the door, hugging her like she's a delicate piece of china, ready to crack at any moment. Her mother's boyfriend, Stan, is waiting at the car. He, at least, hugs Lacie with a little more spirit and then swings her bag jauntily into the trunk, as if he's picking her up at the airport after a fun weekend getaway.

The car ride to their home is quiet and awkward. "How are you," asks her mother, tentatively.

"I'm not seeing stalkers everywhere and imagining that people are out to get me, if that's what you're asking," Lacie bites back. She just couldn't help herself, but her mother's sharp intake of breath and the deafening silence afterward, make her regret saying it.

LITTLE FOXES

After a little while, Lacie attempts to make up for it by changing the subject. "Dr. Giovatti had some suggestions for helping me rebuild my life and make positive changes."

Her mother perks up a little, but it's Stan who takes the bait. "That sounds interesting. Like what?"

"Well, he suggested a job as a copywriter, because of my interest in English and he said it's usually remote work, which would suit me well."

This sparks her mother's interest and Lacie can even make out a small smile break out over her features. "Sounds perfect," says Stan. "What else?"

Lacie finds herself smiling a little as well. "He suggested that I could get a fresh start by changing my name. I've always liked the name Abby. What do you think?"

The faint smile on her mother's face instantly contorts into an angry scowl. Stan, speechless, closes his mouth shut, with a loud snap. Then, her mother explodes.

Lacie tries to recall the forest wall, as her mother shouts, "What is wrong with your name? Your great aunt was named Lacie. I gave you that name!" For the rest of the ride, Lacie retreats into the depths of her mind, not daring to speak again.

Chapter 104

Abby sits in the waiting room of her dentist's office. The TV hanging in the corner of the room is set to a generic news channel. She normally doesn't pay it any mind, but today, something caught her attention.

A man, in his sixties, is looking into the camera with a pleading expression. A woman around the same age stands next to him with a solemn, tear-stained face. But what catches her attention the most is the name that the reporter interviewing them is saying over and over – Lee Conrad.

The screen says their names are Brian and Marie Fox. The reporter is asking the man and woman how they feel about the recent arrest of Lee Conrad for the 2004 kidnapping and murder of their two daughters, Michelle and Laura. The screen switches to a photo of the two girls. They stand, holding hands, ready for the first day of school. Abby sits forward on the edge of her seat, studying the innocence in their child-like faces.

The picture switches back to the parents. The father is speaking, while the mother sobs quietly beside him. The father's words are lost in the murmur of the crowded waiting room, but the look of brokenness on his face captivates Abby and sears itself into her brain.

She stands slowly and walks out of the waiting room, out of the building. She can't remember driving home, but suddenly she is there, sitting at her computer, googling everything she can about the Fox/Conrad case.

This was after her. It never would've happened if she'd done something- turned him in all those years ago. With every photo, new article, and interview, she lets the guilt wash over her and overtake another part of her- until there is nothing left intact.

Chapter 105

Abby opens her laptop and looks through her search history. The results are alarming. There are tons of searches on not only Oscar and his mom, but also on Lee Conrad, the Fox sisters…and herself. She rubs her throbbing temples. Glimpses come back, like electrical shocks. Her, hunched over her computer in the late, late hours, dredging up a painful past. Her, cutting her newspaper clipping and piecing together cryptic messages, only to mail them to herself. Standing in the darkness. Looking down at Oscar and plotting his demise.

The overload of information is too much for her brain to handle. She slides to the floor and lays slumped in a fetal position, hugging her knees to her chest. Is this why her father killed himself? He must've known that he passed his darkness on to her…and it killed him.

Abby closes her eyes tightly, trying to remember what his face looked like. When she can't, she starts hitting herself on the head over and over.

Maybe her father actually figured this thing out. Maybe death is the only true escape.

Chapter 106

"Ladies and gentlemen of the court, we are here today to determine the guilt and sentencing of this man, Gregory- Lee- Conrad. We heard testimony about other young women who Lee tried to kidnap, some from the very same place that Michelle and Laura Fox were last seen. From Lee's own police interviews, we know that he lured them from that mall and into his van that day in April 2004.

The defense would have you believe that he kidnapped them in order to deliver them to his father and uncle, who are the real villains of this story, but were his father and uncle in Fort Worth, when he abducted and raped another fifteen year old girl and then proceeded to beat the witness of this crime- his girlfriend- punching her in her pregnant stomach?

The answer is no. They were three- thousand miles away, both serving time in separate prisons in Pennsylvania. This is a crime that Lee Conrad committed on his own. He kidnapped Michelle and Laura Fox, taking them away from everyone who loved and cared about them. He took them to his house. His basement. We don't know exactly what happened next, but we do know that they were there. We have eyewitness accounts of them looking drugged. And

LITTLE FOXES

we have DNA evidence. A blood stain – Michelle's blood – in the carpet of Lee Conrad's basement.

We may never know exactly what happened in that basement, but we do know that it resulted in innocent bloodshed and the burning of the remains of ten-year-old Laura Fox in a bonfire in West Virginia.

Let's talk about the lives that were snuffed out. Michelle Fox was a pre-teen with a bright future ahead of her. She was smart and outgoing. She was on the cheerleading squad at her school, and she loved hanging out with her friends…and her little sister. She was just becoming interested in boys her age, but she never got to experience having her first kiss or going to her first dance with one. Those things were taken from her.

Laura fox was only ten. She adored her big sister and, while she was quiet, she had so many interests…so much potential. She loved reading and making up stories. She was also taking gymnastics lessons and she wanted to take up karate. She could have done so many things with her life.

Both of these girls will always be remembered as the beautiful beacons of light that they were. No one can take the time that they spent on this earth from them, or their parents- who are here in this court room, desperately seeking closure, because…Lee Conrad took away their futures."

Chapter 107

Abby stares at the wall. She has removed all of the coats from her closet, so she can clearly see it head on – her obsession. It stares back at her in the form of photos. Lee's photo is in the center. Red yarn reaches out from his photo, like tendrils, leading to the evidence against him and the things that he's destroyed. There is a photo of Detective Davis, Lee's house with the basement, his cousin's property with the bonfire. Then, there are photos of the Fox sisters, beautiful and young. Beyond them is a photo of their parents – from the news program. Their faces are consumed with grief. It is a reminder to Abby of the pure love that some parents have for their children.

Then, there is a photo of her. Twelve years old, sitting on the porch of their old farmhouse. The photo was taken just weeks before it happened. Her face is bright – her skin clean and pure.

Even so, this girl already has damage. She feels unloved. She has less to lose than the two angels below her, or their grieving parents- who lost their world.

LITTLE FOXES

It should have been her. Now she will reset the universe – make it right.

The edges of the room start to blur, and she feels lightheaded, so she lays down on the floor. She lifts the phone to her ear. It seems to ring forever, but then, there is a click and the familiar pitch of her mother's anxious voice. "Lacie, are you okay?"

"Lacie is dead, mom. She died when she was twelve years old and a man – a monster – raped her in the back of a dirty van and then left her for dead. But her husk of a body kept going, kept living, even though no one cared enough to help bring her back to life."

Abby pauses. Her mom is silent on the other end of the phone – speechless, for once. "It was his baby – the monster's. The one that you made me get rid of and then forget. I guess it's for the best, though. Even God wouldn't have loved it, right?

I think my father was right. This world is not made for people like us. So, I fixed it. It's time for the husk to die too. I just wanted you to know that I don't blame you. You are the only person who ever sort of loved me."

Abby clicks the end button, cutting off her mother's voice. She stares at the closet wall – at the little girl she used to be. Then she closes her eyes.

Chapter 108

Abby stands still in the darkness. She knows this place – she's been here before. She walks slowly, as if she's being drawn forward by some invisible force. Dead leaves and twigs stick to her bare feet.

The van sits in the clearing and she knows what's inside. There is a spotlight on it, surrounding it in a perfect circle of light. Everything else around her fades to black and she knows what she must do.

She walks up to the back doors of the van. She begins lifting her arm, but at that moment, the door swings open. She is suddenly face to face with her twelve-year-old self.

They both freeze, stunned – somehow knowing one another, and not knowing each other at all. Then, there is a slight movement in the darkness behind the girl. Shoulders lift…and then that one desperate word in that pathetic voice. "Lacie?"

Abby looks herself square in the face. "Run," she says, and the girl takes off with a resolve that she didn't know she had. Abby steps back a little, readying herself for what is coming next.

LITTLE FOXES

She closes her eyes and feels the anger coursing through her veins. When she opens them, he is there. He looks at her with a quizzical expression. "Where is Lacie?"

"I am Lacie."

Realization dawns on him and he readies himself for attack, knowing that this is inevitable. He pulls his leg back into a sprint position and then takes off.

Lacie plants her feet. When he is about to tackle her she goes up on her tiptoes and ballet twirls around him. When he straightens up and looks around, confused, she punches him right in the lower spine. The crunch is audible, and he flies forward, his back bending at a painful angle. He face-plants into the ground.

He lifts himself up with a groan, and spits blood onto the ground. Lacie takes the opportunity to switch to attack mode. She runs toward him. He, however, can sense her presence. He jumps up onto his feet, poised in a crouching position, and then does a backflip.

His move puts him farther away from her, throwing off her trajectory, but not for long. She adjusts by running up a nearby tree and then springing off, by pushing her feet against the trunk. She spirals through the air towards him like a missile. This time she will not miss.

LITTLE FOXES

She collides into him, pushing him forward, like a sled, through the forest bed. He grabs her head, holding it to his chest and making it so she can't see where they are going. All of a sudden, he rolls them onto their sides and releases, pushing himself away from her. She doesn't see the tree until right before she smashes into it.

She only has time to turn herself so that her leg takes the brunt of the blow, rather than her head. Pain sears through her leg, like stabbing knives. It brings tears to her eyes.

Then, He laughs from somewhere, a few feet away and it fuels her anger, like a rush of sugar and cocaine. It's time to end this.

She stands and faces him. Her leg seems to be bending the wrong way and she can't put pressure on it, but she still has arms and another good leg.

She looks around, spotting what she is looking for. A large rock, jutting out of the ground with sharp, jagged edges. She hops towards it, acting like she's running away - trying to escape. He takes the bait. He follows her and when he's close enough, she does a side cartwheel, away from him.

He doesn't see the rock. He barrels forward, tripping on it. It rips his pants, tearing off chunks of his leg as he goes down. He lies on the ground, holding his mutilated leg and screaming in pain.

LITTLE FOXES

Lacie hobbles over to him. She bends down and wrenches the rock from the ground. She stands over him with the rock in her arm, ready to smash it against his face. But something stops her.

As she looks down at him, her perception clears, and she can suddenly see him for what he truly is. Not a monster, but a sniveling coward. Emotions flood over her all at once. She was a child. She didn't ask for anything that happened.

"IT'S NOT MY FAULT!" She screams the words into the night air, like she's expelling a demon. Something leaves with them – her anger. She drops the rock and walks away, ignoring his sad, pleading sobs behind her.

The sirens and red flashing lights greet her beyond the edge of the woods. She doesn't know what will happen when she walks towards them, but she does know that it's better than living in the past.

Chapter 109

She sips her coffee- black and strong – as usual. A lot has changed over the past few months, but some things never will. Every day is a struggle. She has to push herself to get out of bed in the morning and she's back on her medication, but…it's getting easier.

Therapy has helped her tremendously. Although some days are harder than others, she is actively practicing giving herself grace, while also holding herself accountable to learn from her mistakes.

Now, as she sips her coffee, she contemplates the past year. She thinks about Oscar. He did not in any way deserve the treatment she gave him. They have not spoken since that day in the parking lot, and she knows that he is most likely out there somewhere thinking that she is a crazy Bitch. And maybe she is, but she hopes that one day she'll be able to apologize and thank him for being so nice. She also hopes that someday she'll be able to maintain a healthy relationship with someone and reciprocate that kindness.

For now, though, she is focusing on herself and her mental health, which means taking things one day at a time. If there is one thing she now knows though for certain, it's that she doesn't want to die. That night was the best and worst night of her life, and she came very close. Her mom had apparently called an ambulance. They burst into her apartment and brought her back to life. And she will forever be grateful for that.

Her cell phone buzzes, and she answers it. "Okay, see you soon." A few minutes later, the doorbell rings. She opens the door to her mother - brown paper bags, teetering precariously in her arms.

"The farmers market was having a great sale. I just couldn't help myself! I thought maybe we could cook together today, instead of going out."

She takes the bags from her mom and places them on the counter. Then, they hug. She has realized that, even though her mother hasn't always been emotionally present, she did the best she could – under the circumstances. And, she has always been there for her. They are working on an open communicative relationship. Her mom told her that her father tried to hide his struggles from them both and she was so in love with him that she was blinded to it. When he died, she thought she would never get over him. She was also so angry at him for leaving her that she just couldn't talk about it. But Lacie, in her youthful ambivalence, just kept asking what had happened to her dad. She thought replacing him, with anyone, would help fill the hole left, for them both. When she met Stan many years later, her heart began to thaw, and she realized that it was possible for her to fall in love again.

They haven't talked a lot about the rape. Her mother admitted that she knew something had happened, but she was too scared and still too numb to be able to face it. Her mom's face still contorts with a look of anguish and fear every time she brings it up, but she doesn't shut her out anymore and they are working on pushing through the guilt and discomfort...together.

Right on cue a fluffy orange cat jumps onto the kitchen counter, rubbing its face and body slowly across all of the shopping bags. "Oh, you silly boy", her mother exclaims.

His name is Calcifer and she loved him the moment she saw him. She saw an ad in a newspaper while she was in the clinic. Cell phones and computers were off limits while she was letting her mind and body rest, but newspapers, magazines and books were allowed. It was kind of nice to go old-school for a while. Something drew her to the ad. It had read, Free kitten, found abandoned in a ditch. She called the man immediately to see if the kitten was still available.

"He is," he said in a scratchy old man drawl. "Poor little fella, didn't think he would make it to be honest. When I found him, he was wet, shivering and covered in dried blood. Some people have come to look at him but, well...he's got six toes on both his front paws and his tail kind of curls upward onto his back. I think it kinda throws folks off a little."

She already knew she wanted him. She sent her mom to go see him and she came in to visit her the next day, with special permission from her doctor to show her a video on her phone. It was love at first sight.

"I want him," she had said with tears brimming in her eyes.

"I figured," her mom had said. "That's why I brought him home with me."

Now, she grabs a hold of the fluffy cat and buries her face in his soft fur. He is already becoming a full-sized cat. He has grown into his paws, which used to look like catcher's mitts on his tiny body, and his tail has become full and fluffy, spiraling on his back like a husky tail. People constantly comment on how pretty and interesting he looks now. His fur is a fiery orange, and she swears sometimes he makes that face that calcifer makes in Howls Moving Castle when he's about to be extinguished, hence the name. He is her comfort and her joy.

The trial, the thing which had consumed her life for a long time, came and went. She missed the verdict as she was too busy having a breakdown, but she did look into it while she was in the hospital. Gregory, Lee, Conrad was found guilty of both the kidnapping and murders of Michelle and Laura Fox. He is currently serving two

LITTLE FOXES

consecutive life sentences. He will die in prison. She cried when she got out and looked it up on her computer and saw the footage of Brian and Marie Fox crying and praising God in the courtroom. It will never make up for losing their daughters, of course, but justice was served. The thought does offer some comfort, but she has come to realize that it isn't her closure. She got her closure that night in the woods, the night she almost died. When she forgave herself and let go of her anger.

Not that she would recommend the method to anyone who asks. She had to get her stomach pumped and then she was sent to the hospital's psychiatric ward, which is definitely no walk in the park. Hurting people yelled and screamed around her every day, trying to express their anguish. Then, she was released and checked in to an in-patient mental health clinic, where she had to learn to do the work that it took to rebuild her strength, both mentally and physically. There are some pretty nasty side effects to a pill induced suicide attempt, ranging from severe headaches to loss of motor functions to full on seizures. It has been a scary road getting here, and there is still road left before her. For the first time in a long time though, she feels as though she is not alone.

"I love you Abb- I mean Lacie, my beautiful Lacie," says her mother, lovingly stroking her cheek.

"I love you too, mom."

LITTLE FOXES

<u>Aknowledgements</u>

<u>I would like recognize my family, especially my husband for pushing me to do things that I might never have done without their encouragement. They are my support system, which is something that I very much need.</u>

<u>I would also like to take a moment to talk about all the real missing, abused and murdered children of this world. This story is dark because darkness exists. I can't even begin to express my admiration for all of the detectives and just plain decent human beings out there who are consumed with the need to do something about it. To those people, I raise my hat and say, "you are the best of us".</u>

LITTLE FOXES